VANCOUVER NIGHTMARE

Books by Eric Wilson

The Tom and Liz Austen Mysteries

1. Murder on *The Canadian*
2. Vancouver Nightmare
3. The Ghost of Lunenburg Manor
4. Disneyland Hostage
5. The Kootenay Kidnapper
6. Vampires of Ottawa
7. Spirit in the Rainforest
8. The Green Gables Detectives
9. Code Red at the Supermall
10. Cold Midnight in Vieux Québec
11. The Ice Diamond Quest
12. The Prairie Dog Conspiracy
13. The St. Andrews Werewolf

Also available by Eric Wilson

Summer of Discovery
The Unmasking of 'Ksan
Terror in Winnipeg
Lost Treasure of Casa Loma

Vancouver Nightmare

ERIC WILSON

Illustrated by
TOM McNEELY

HarperCollins*Publishers*Ltd

First published in hardcover by Clarke, Irwin & Company
Limited and The Bodley Head (Canada) Ltd: 1978
First paperback edition: 1982

Canadian Cataloguing in Publication Data

Wilson, Eric
  Vancouver nightmare

(A Tom Austen mystery)
ISBN 0-00-222631-6

I. McNeely, Tom. II. Title.

PS8595.I4793V35 1982   jC813'.54   C82-094965-5
PZ7.W55Va 1982

93 94 95 96 97 98 99 OFF 10 9 8 7 6 5 4 3

For Bob Linnell

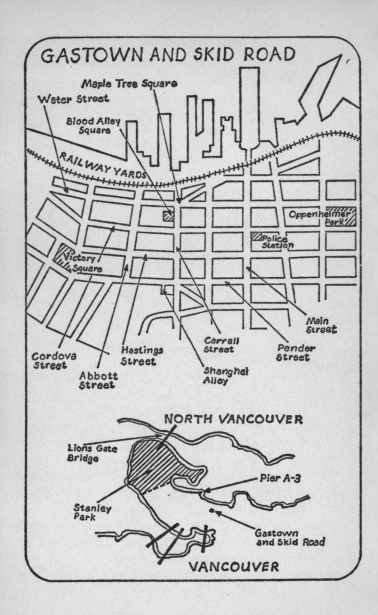

1

The coffin was open, the air black and musty all around.

With a pounding heart, Tom stepped close and saw the body of Count Dracula, his head on a satin pillow. Straining his eyes through the darkness, Tom saw blood on the vampire's teeth.

Without warning, Dracula began to move.

At first he only shuddered. But then, suddenly and swiftly, Dracula sat straight up, his terrible blood-stained fangs reaching for Tom's throat.

With a cry of fear, Tom jumped back. At the same moment, to his great relief, Dracula settled back and his head returned to rest on the satin pillow.

His body trembling, Tom turned to Dietmar. 'This

7

place spooks me,' he whispered. 'Let's get out of here.'

Dietmar nodded, and together they ran up the stairs and stepped outside into hot sunshine. Above their heads, a sign read: *Gastown Wax Museum . . . Visit The Chamber of Horrors!!*

Dietmar laughed. 'That was fantastic, Austen. When Dracula sat up, you almost jumped out of your skin.'

'No way,' Tom said, blushing under his freckles. 'It takes more than a mechanical monster to scare me, Oban.'

'Then let's go back. I didn't get a good look at the Space Creature.'

'Forget it,' Tom said, 'I'm hungry. Anyway, there's my grandparents.'

The two walked up the street towards a white-haired couple, who were examining leather belts on a push-cart.

'Hi, Nanny and Gramps,' Tom said. 'The Chamber of Horrors was great, especially when they asked to put Dietmar on display.'

Nanny smiled. 'We've another treat for you.'

'Terrific!' said Dietmar.

Gramps studied the tourists wandering around Maple Tree Square, then took Nanny's hand and led the way along Water Street.

'Until recently,' he said, pointing at the street's brick buildings, 'these boutiques were just Skid Road flop joints. Then the area was redeveloped and named Gastown.'

'What's Skid Road mean?' Dietmar asked.

'It's an old logging expression. In pioneer days, cheap hotels stood beside the roads along which logs were "skidded" to the sawmills. So the poor part of cities like Vancouver and Seattle became known as Skid Road.'

'Gastown doesn't look very poor to me.'

'It's not any more, but Vancouver still has a Skid Road, just beyond those buildings.'

'Skid Road sounds neat,' Tom said. 'I'd love to explore there.'

Gramps shook his head. 'That's not a good idea, Tom.'

'Why not?'

'To start with, there's a lot of criminals in that area.'

'Fantastic!' Tom said. 'Maybe I could find a mystery to solve.'

Nanny smiled at her husband. 'Now you've said the wrong thing, Bob. You know Tom thinks only of being a detective.'

Gramps nodded. 'I guess that was a mistake. Well, here's our treat, a meal at The Breadline.'

'Bread?' Tom said, disappointed. 'That sounds like a prison meal.' Pausing to note the location of Skid Road, he followed his grandparents into the restaurant. The air smelled of freshly baked bread, and honky-tonk music came from an old-fashioned player-piano; on the walls hung ancient toasters, pots and pans, even a rickety sewing machine.

The hostess led them to a corner table, and handed out small newspapers. 'Weird,' Dietmar said, sitting down. 'What kind of place is this?'

'During the Depression people were terribly poor,' Nanny explained, 'and many had to stand in a "breadline" to get free food.'

Tom studied his newspaper, which was actually the restaurant's menu. 'I think I'll have some Hard-Times Chicken Noodle Soup.'

'I'll have strawberry shortcake,' Dietmar said, 'then

9

deep-dish blueberry cobbler, oatmeal raisin cookies and a few cinnamon rolls.'

Tom looked at his smiling grandparents. 'Don't laugh,' he said. 'Dietmar isn't exactly fat, but he's the champ at pigging out.'

'Now, Tom, be polite,' said Nanny. 'Dietmar is our guest.'

After their orders had been taken, Gramps asked a riddle. 'Why did Sherlock Holmes know that a train had passed a certain place?'

Tom scratched his head. 'I should know that one.'

'Because the train left its tracks behind.'

Tom smiled with affection at his grandparents. He was having a good summer holiday with them, but now he'd discovered the perfect way to find some real excitement.

He would investigate Skid Road for crime.

The thought was so exciting, Tom didn't think he could eat. But each person received a miniature loaf of whole wheat bread, and his mouth watered. 'I think I could live on bread and water,' he said happily. 'Prison can't be too bad.'

Gramps shook his head. 'I understand prison is a grim life, and very boring. It's true that crime doesn't pay.'

Nanny smiled at Tom. 'Speaking of crime, do you read detective books?'

'You bet. I've read everything possible about analysing clues, following suspects, that sort of thing.'

'But how do you find suspects to follow?'

'There are criminals everywhere,' Tom said. He looked around the restaurant, then lowered his voice. 'Look at those men who just came in. If that fat one isn't a crook, I'll eat my hat.'

All eyes swung to the entrance, where two men were discussing the player-piano. One, dressed in a business suit, was Japanese; the other also wore a suit, but it was badly rumpled and a big pot belly hung over the man's belt. His thin hair was combed straight back over a pink scalp.

'Disgusting,' Tom said. 'Look at that double chin, quivering like a turkey's wattle.'

As Tom spoke, the man's eyes narrowed and he started in their direction.

'He heard you!' Dietmar whispered. 'I think he's going to shoot us, and there's nowhere to hide!'

'Don't be silly,' Tom said, his voice shaking. 'That only happens on TV.'

As the man reached their table he suddenly held out his hand and Tom jumped, expecting a pistol to blaze. Instead, the man shook hands with Gramps. 'I thought I recognized you, Bob,' he said.

'How are you, Inspector?' Gramps asked. 'I believe you remember my wife Eve, and these two young gentlemen are from Winnipeg. Tom is our grandson, and Dietmar is staying with his relatives in North Vancouver.'

Tom's face was scarlet. 'Inspector?' he said, in a feeble voice.

'That's right. Inspector Mort, of the Vancouver City Police.'

Dietmar roared with laughter, and even Tom's grandparents grinned. Tom felt like crawling under the table.

'What's the joke?' Inspector Mort asked. 'This guy's face is as red as his hair.'

Dietmar chuckled gleefully. 'We've just had a brilliant lesson in crime-busting from Tom Austen, the defective detective.'

'A detective?'

11

'That's right,' Gramps said. 'Inspector, why don't you and your friend join us?'

'All right.' Inspector Mort beckoned to the second man, who came to the table. 'This is Captain Yakashi, of the freighter *M K Maru*. He's assisting me with a case while his ship is docked in Vancouver.'

Tom studied the captain's handsome face, disappointed he didn't have tattooes and a gold ear-ring. Was he really a captain? Tom was tempted to wring out the truth with a few questions, but he didn't want to risk looking foolish a second time. Instead, he looked at Inspector Mort.

'What case are you on?' he asked timidly.

The Inspector turned a grumpy face to Tom. 'That's a pretty personal question, young man.'

Tom blushed again, and Dietmar giggled.

Gramps gave Tom a smile. 'Don't be too hard on Tom, Inspector. He's fascinated by police work.'

'Sorry,' the Inspector said gruffly. 'Well, son, it's a complicated case involving illegal immigrants from the Orient, but I can't give details.'

Gramps smiled. 'That's a good cover story, Inspector, but now tell us the truth. Aren't you really after all those drugs being smuggled into Vancouver on freighters from the Orient?'

There was a long silence, while the Inspector stared at Tom's grandfather. 'Nobody believes the police these days.'

Gramps looked embarrassed. 'Now it's my turn to apologize.' He waited for the waitress to put down their soup, then turned to the Inspector. 'We were just discussing what prison life must be like. Could Tom tour your police cells? I know he'd be thrilled.'

Another silence, and Tom thought Inspector Mort

must have regretted choosing The Breadline for lunch. But the man surprised Tom by smiling, revealing a collection of big teeth. 'Sure, son, I'll show you round.'

Tom thanked the Inspector and turned to the soup, not wanting to tempt fate by asking about the drug smuggling, even though he ached to know more. When he had cleaned up his plate he looked at his grandparents.

'May Dietmar and I poke around Gastown?'

After a moment's hesitation, permission was granted. Inspector Mort made arrangements with Tom about the tour of the cells, good-byes were said, and the boys found themselves back in the sunshine.

'I noticed a hobby shop earlier,' Dietmar said. 'Let's go and look around.'

'I've got a better idea.' Tom took out a map of Gastown. 'How about finding some crooks?'

'Crooks like Inspector Wart?'

'His name is Inspector Mort, and that was a mistake.' Tom dropped his voice to an excited whisper. 'Listen, Dietmar, it's obvious the Inspector is searching Gastown for drug smugglers. If we can find them first, we'll be heroes!'

Dietmar shook his head. 'I'm too young to die.'

'Don't be a Nervous Nelly.' Tom pointed to his map. 'Here's a place called Blood Alley Square. That sounds perfect for a stake out.'

When Dietmar hesitated, Tom grabbed his arm and they started walking, 'I'll protect you,' he promised. 'This will be a great adventure.'

'I need an adventure like I need a hole in the head,' Dietmar muttered. 'Let's forget the crooks and spend our money on some candy.'

Tom dragged Dietmar into a doorway. 'I'm glad you

13

mentioned money,' he whispered, getting out his cash. Quickly, he slipped off his shoe and put the money inside. 'Do the same with yours so it won't be lost if we're mugged.'

'*Mugged?*' Dietmar stared at Tom, his brown eyes wide. 'I quit.'

Nervous about facing Blood Alley Square alone, Tom managed a grin. 'I'm just kidding. Come on, there's nothing to fear.'

'Except having our ribs tickled by a knife.'

'Not a chance.'

After some twisting passageways, they emerged into a courtyard with cobblestones and maple trees. 'It's not creepy enough,' Tom said unhappily. He pointed to a bench. 'Let's sit down and see what we get.'

'Two sore rear ends,' Dietmar predicted, 'and maybe headaches as a bonus.'

But Dietmar was wrong. After a few minutes of watching tourists wander through the square, Tom sat up and grabbed Dietmar's arm. 'Look!'

'What?'

'Over there, but don't stare.' Tom flicked his eyes towards a passageway, where a man of about thirty, his head and beard a mass of curly black hair, was staring at the sky.

'That's our man,' Tom said.

'Why him?'

'Can't you see he's looking straight at the sun? Only a drug addict could do that, and not roast his eyeballs.'

'Are you sure?' Dietmar said doubtfully.

'Sure I'm sure.' Tom watched carefully, his suspicions confirmed when the man scratched vigorously at his hair and beard. 'He's got lice, from sleeping in opium dens.'

14

The man reached into his shabby jeans and threw some fluff into the air, laughing as it floated away on the breeze. Then he scratched his beard again and looked at the sun, licking his lips.

'Nutty as a fruitcake,' Tom whispered.

'Yeah, a real weirdo,' Dietmar agreed. 'Let's go home.'

'Not when he could lead us straight to the smugglers.' Tom leaned forward in excitement as the man crossed the square and disappeared into a narrow alley. 'We can't let him escape!'

Reluctantly, Dietmar followed Tom into the alley. At the far end they saw traffic, but the man was gone.

'Hurry!'

They ran to the end of the alley and then stopped short, amazed by the scene before their eyes.

'It's Skid Road!' Tom said, thrilled.

Old buildings frowned down, their walls streaked with dirt. Above doorways, battered signs read WESTERN POOL HALL and BEER PARLOUR. In the air was the noise and smell of the cars and trucks streaming past.

'Wow, this is great,' Tom said. 'And, look, there's the Scratcher.'

Along the street, the bearded man stood talking to a woman wearing a purple blouse, red skirt and silver high-heeled shoes. As Tom and Dietmar watched, the Scratcher moved off. Before they could follow, a voice called: 'Hey, boys.'

At an open window above, a bleary-eyed face with several missing teeth was leaning out. 'Seen my cat, boys?'

Tom shook his head, and they moved on.

'What a strange man,' Dietmar whispered.

15

'I thought it was a woman.' Tom looked into an abandoned building, its floor littered with broken bottles, then stared at an approaching man who wore a length of chain instead of a belt. 'This place is a bonanza!' he said. 'Everyone looks like a criminal.'

The Scratcher was waiting for a traffic light. Tom took out his notebook to write a description of the man and note they had reached the corner of Cordova and Abbott.

Dietmar watched anxiously. 'If a crook sees you making notes, you'll be killed,' he warned.

'That doesn't worry me,' Tom said. 'But our good clothes make us stick out like sore thumbs.'

'I'll go home and change,' Dietmar said quickly, turning back.

'Oh no, you don't.' Tom took a firm grip on Dietmar's arm. 'Look, our man is moving. After him!'

The Scratcher walked quickly to Hastings Street, then headed west. After a block, he turned abruptly into a dark passage and disappeared. Tom hesitated, then went nervously down the passage to a door. It was locked.

Out of nowhere, a man's voice spoke: 'Looking for something?'

Startled, Tom looked left and saw a window. Behind it, a red-moustached man sat with a newspaper, a cigar in his mouth. His eyes were unfriendly as he stared at Tom.

'Uh,' Tom said, trying to think, 'uh, my father said to meet him here.'

The man sucked on his cigar, then exhaled a cloud of dirty grey smoke and gestured towards the street with the cigar's soggy butt. 'This is a private club,' he said. 'Beat it, little man.'

'But . . .'

'Beat it.'

'Yes, sir.' Tom walked slowly back to the street, where Dietmar stood grinning.

'Curses,' Dietmar said, 'foiled again.'

'Drop on your head.' Tom made some notes, then he and Dietmar set off towards Gastown. Although Tom's investigation had been a dud so far, he felt good as he made a secret vow.

He would return to Skid Road.

2

Two days later, Tom sat in a battered car driven by Inspector Mort.

A jagged crack ran across one window, the brown seat covers were stained, and dust rose from the floor, which was littered with old milkshake containers. It was a depressing view of Inspector Mort's life.

As the officer stopped the car in a parking lot, he yawned and scratched his large stomach.

'Let's go, son,' he said, getting out of the car and starting towards a building with squad cars and police motorcycles parked outside. 'If you get arrested this summer, you'll be brought in this door for booking.'

'Why would I be arrested, Inspector?'

The fat man shrugged. 'There's lots of runaway kids in Vancouver, getting into trouble.' He led the way to an elevator; as it rose up inside the building, Tom noticed that someone had written on the wall: *A new day bang bang you're dead.*

Stepping out, Tom saw metal doors and a long corridor which smelled of bleach. A uniformed man, holding a ring of enormous keys, saluted Inspector Mort.

'Show him around, would you?' the Inspector said, gesturing at Tom.

'Yes, sir.'

Inspector Mort went into an office and poured himself a coffee. As Tom followed the warder, he heard a piercing whistle.

'That's Charlie you hear,' the warder said, smiling. 'He's waiting to be taken to the nut-house. Meanwhile, he's been eating our paper cups and decorating his cell with toilet paper.'

Another whistle echoed down the concrete corridor.

'Look in here,' the warder said, indicating a steel door with a small window. 'We call this guy Tiger.'

Tom saw a young man pacing back and forth; his hair was rumpled, his open shirt exposed a red scar, and he stopped to look at Tom with angry eyes. Tom stepped back nervously, and the man resumed his pacing.

'He scares me,' Tom said. 'His eyes are so mean.'

'He is mean,' the warder said. 'He's a drug pusher, and he's under arrest for murder.'

Tom shivered, suddenly missing the safe world outside. As he glanced down the corridor, Inspector Mort came out of the office.

'Give me your keys,' he said to the warder.

Selecting a large key, Inspector Mort opened an

empty cell. 'Go on in and see what it's like,' he said to Tom.

Slowly Tom walked into the cell, looking at the initials scratched into the grey paint by prisoners. Behind him, the door clanged shut and he heard the key grind in the lock. Frightened, Tom turned to see Inspector Mort walking away.

'Hey!' he called. 'What's going on?'

There was no reply. Tom tried to open the door, then stepped back in shock. He had been tricked, led straight into a trap. But why?

There was another shrieking whistle from Charlie, and Tom covered his ears with sweating hands. What should he do? He looked desperately for a means of escape, then walked on trembling legs to the steel bunk and sat down, trying to think.

A moment later, Inspector Mort appeared at the cell and opened the door. 'How do you like being a prisoner?' he asked, twirling the ring of keys in his hand.

Tom looked at the man, unable to answer.

'Come on, son,' said Inspector Mort, leaving the cell. 'I hope this sample of prison life will keep you out of trouble.'

Tom went into the corridor, unable to think of anything but getting away from the Inspector. Still trembling, he followed him to the office, where a handsome young officer was holding a coffee cup.

Inspector Mort looked at the officer. 'This youngster is a little green around the gills from being locked up, Bud, so how about buying him a Coke?'

'Sure, Inspector.' Bud gave Tom a friendly smile, and shook his hand. As they started towards the elevator, Inspector Mort closed the office door with a bang.

Bud laughed. 'Don't mind the Inspector, Tom. He

spends so much time being called a pig by arrested kids that he thinks there aren't any nice kids around. He can be a good guy, too.'

'I guess so,' Tom said, remembering the Inspector had troubled to arrange a tour. But was this done out of kindness, or so the man could throw a scare into him? Thinking about the motive for the Inspector's strange behaviour was puzzling, and Tom didn't begin to relax until he was outside in the sunshine.

'Still want that Coke?' Bud asked, then laughed. 'Trust the Inspector not to supply the money. He's always short of cash.'

'I can pay,' Tom offered, but Bud shook his head and led the way across Main Street to a small building with a sign by the door reading: *Members and Guests Only.*

The interior was dark and cool, with people sitting around low tables. There were pictures on the walls, and a small bar.

'This is the Police Club, for off-duty officers,' Bud said. 'I'll get us a couple of Cokes.'

A man sitting alone smiled at Tom and pointed to some empty chairs at his side. The man, who had blond hair and a blond beard, stood up as Tom approached and held out a big hand. 'Hi, I'm Harrison Walsh,' he said, squeezing Tom's hand in a powerful grip.

Tom introduced himself, and sat down. Despite having had his hand nearly squashed, he liked the relaxed appearance of the man in his jeans and open shirt, at his throat a silver medallion on a leather thong.

Bud appeared with two drinks. 'Hiya, Harrison,' he said, sitting down and rolling back his shirt cuffs, revealing blue tattooes. 'How's things?'

'Too busy.'

'Harrison and I were together on the motorcycle

squad,' Bud explained to Tom. 'Then Harrison decided he wanted more money, and quit the Force.'

'What do you do now?' Tom asked.

'I'm a youth worker. I help young kids and teenagers who are mixed up with drugs.'

'Harrison doesn't have an easy assignment,' Bud added.

'We face a big problem, Tom, especially when kids are forced into crime to pay for drugs.'

Bud's face was troubled. 'Once they're hooked, those kids are at the mercy of ruthless drug pushers who will do anything, even commit murder, to protect their operation.'

'That sounds horrible,' said Tom.

Bud nodded. 'But it's all too true, I'm afraid. Only this morning we found the body of a police agent washed up at Pier A-3. He must have been getting close to some key people in the Vancouver drug trade, so they murdered him.'

Harrison looked at Bud. 'Who was the agent?'

'A young recruit who was working undercover on Skid Road. His name was Brian Atkinson.'

'No!' Harrison said, looking shocked. 'I sat right here with Brian earlier this week, and talked about his under-cover assignment. He can't be dead?'

'I'm afraid so,' Bud said.

'Maybe Tiger killed him,' Tom suggested.

'That guy in the cells?' Bud shook his head. 'Impossible, since he's been under arrest for several days.'

Harrison looked at Tom. 'Did someone show you round the cells?'

'Yes, Inspector Wart did.' The men laughed at the joke and Tom glowed with pleasure, happy he'd brightened their spirits. It was great to be with them, listening to their conversation about police activities.

'You must enjoy doing patrol work,' Tom said to Bud, hoping to hear more about his life as a motorcycle policeman.

'You're right,' Bud said, 'but it gets depressing when motorists blow their tops because they're caught breaking the law.'

Harrison shook his head. 'Some people are crazy,' he said. 'Once I was in a shoot-out with a man holed up at a window with a rifle. I was sheltering behind a telephone pole, with bullets whizzing past, and people were standing across the street, watching.'

'But there are funny moments,' Bud said. 'Last week I was called to the Bus Depot, and found a man standing there in his underwear. He'd been mugged, and the crooks had taken everything, even his clothes.'

Tom reached for his Coke. 'It sounds like a neat life.'

Bud smiled. 'I bet you'd enjoy a spin on my police motorcycle, but it's against the rules.' Turning, he looked at Harrison. 'Got your motorcycle here?'

'Sure do,' Harrison said. He smiled at Tom, and got out a packet of Old Port cigars. 'Let me have a smoke, then we'll go for a ride.'

'Great, thanks!' With the upset of being locked in a cell now forgotten, Tom felt completely relaxed. 'Say,' he asked, 'do you know why some governments don't hang criminals with wooden legs?'

There was a puzzled silence, while Tom grinned. 'Because they use rope!'

Laughing, Bud finished his drink and crunched the ice cubes in his teeth. 'I've got something interesting here.'

Tom leaned forward as Bud took out a round steel

23

object with jagged teeth. 'It looks like a star,' Tom said. 'What's it for?'

'Killing,' Bud answered casually. 'It's an Oriental weapon. called a Shuriken. Thrown with a flick of the wrist, it can be super deadly.'

Tom studied the vicious object, wondering how Bud could be so nonchalant about it, but perhaps that came from being involved with criminals every day. 'Where did you get it?' he asked.

'An investigation,' Bud said. 'That reminds me, I must get back to duty, Tom, but perhaps we'll meet again.'

'That would be great.'

Bud ripped the cover off a packet of matches, and wrote a phone number on the back. 'This is my number,' he said. 'Call me sometime, and we'll have another Coke.'

'Thanks,' Tom said, smiling happily.

When Bud had left, Harrison picked up a motorcycle helmet and they went to the back lane, where a big Harley-Davidson was parked.

Harrison put on silver-coated sunglasses, and Tom's excited face was reflected in their lenses. 'I keep an extra helmet in here,' Harrison said, opening a saddle bag. 'It should fit you fine.'

The helmet smelled of leather and sweat. Tom felt great as he did up its strap and climbed on to the motorcycle behind Harrison, wishing his friends could see him.

With a roar they were off, shooting towards the end of the lane. Startled pigeons fluttered into the air, and a man jumped aside as they picked up speed.

Tom was aware of green leaves, and had a glimpse of Maple Tree Square before they were flying along Water

Street. Harrison swung to the left, the motorcycle leaned close to the road, and Tom tightened his grip as the machine found more power in its booming engine.

Harrison turned his head. 'Fun?' he yelled.

'Great!' Tom shouted, the word almost lost in the wind that tore at his face.

Harrison sped quickly past other traffic, and too soon they were back on Main Street with the police station ahead. Then they were stopped by a red light.

'Let's spin down to the docks,' Harrison said.

Tom smiled happily. Again the engine roared and his head snapped back as they took off with a screech of rubber, heading north towards the docks.

The salty smell of sea air came to Tom as the harbour appeared, sunlight glittering on its blue waters and gulls floating above it on warm currents of air. As Harrison cut the engine, the piercing cries of the beautiful white birds could be heard.

'What a scene!' said Tom, staring across the harbour to North Vancouver, where houses climbed up a wall of mountains. Then a seaplane appeared, and glided down to land lightly on the waves.

'Where's Pier A-3?' Tom asked.

'That way,' Harrison said, pointing along the harbour front. 'Why do you ask?'

'Oh, no special reason,' Tom said, too shy to mention his idea of investigating the pier for clues about the murder of the police undercover agent.

Harrison started the engine and they took off in another burst of speed. Reaching Main Street, they pulled in under a SHELL sign and stopped by the pumps. As Harrison fumbled with the cap of his fuel tank, Tom stood up, stretching his muscles.

'Thanks for the fantastic ride,' he said. 'I can walk from here.'

Harrison smiled. 'Maybe I'll see you again.'

'Could we go for another ride?'

'Good idea. Where's that paper with Bud's phone number?' Tom got it out, and Harrison added his own number.

'Where do you live?' Tom asked.

'In a houseboat near the Bayshore Inn.'

'Neat!' Tom said. 'I'd love to see it.'

Harrison laughed. 'It's only a little shack, but phone me sometime and we'll arrange a visit.'

'Thanks!' Tom said. He hung around as Harrison fuelled the motorcycle, not wanting the good time to end. But when a teenage girl of about sixteen came out of a washroom in the Shell station and started towards them, Harrison squeezed Tom's arm.

'One of my customers,' he said. 'You'd better go, Tom.'

'Sure.' Tom looked at the girl, whose greasy hair hung limply beside her lifeless face. She looked pathetic, holding a cigarette in skinny fingers as she walked shakily towards the motorcycle, and Tom realized how big a problem Harrison faced in his work.

Saying good-bye, Tom started back to the police station, thinking about the murdered police agent and his idea of searching Pier A-3 for clues. The plan made him nervous, but it might lead to valuable information about the Vancouver drug trade. If so, it would be worth the risk.

3

On Sunday, the boys and Tom's grandparents decided to visit Stanley Park. Dietmar did not enjoy the walk along the sea wall that winds around it.

'I've got blisters on my blisters,' he said, wiping his forehead. 'I'm sure we've been walking for hours.'

Nanny smiled. 'Keep on trudging, Dietmar, then you and Tom can have something to eat.'

Dietmar cheered up, and looked at the nearby bridge that stretched from a bluff far above their heads across to the distant shore. 'Is that a restaurant up on the bridge?'

'No,' Nanny said. 'It's a look-out booth for directing ships in and out of the harbour.'

Rounding a bend, they came to a small lighthouse. Parked on the sea wall was a repair truck marked *Transport Canada*, and Tom saw several men eating their lunches. To his surprise, Inspector Mort sat with the men.

Gramps, too, was surprised. 'Hello there, Inspector!' he said. 'Why are you here?'

'I've been enjoying a walk,' the Inspector said in his gruff voice, 'and stopped to chat with this repair crew.'

One of the men smiled. 'He's been keeping us busy with his questions, not to mention eating our sandwiches.'

Gramps laughed. 'Why are you working on a Sunday? That seems odd.'

The man gestured towards the lighthouse. 'The foghorn is out of order, so it must be repaired immediately. Trouble is, we can't figure out what's wrong.'

'I've made some suggestions,' Inspector Mort said. 'Broken machines are more interesting than broken people.'

'Well,' Gramps said, 'we'd better be off.'

As Tom walked away, he noticed the Inspector and the men remained silent until they were alone again. Then he turned to look up at the deck of the bridge, far above his head.

'Is that the Golden Gate Bridge?' he asked.

'Wrong city,' said Gramps, looking annoyed at Tom's poor geography. 'This is the Lions Gate Bridge.'

'Oops,' Tom said, 'I think I made a boo-boo.' To make up for his mistake, he tried to think of something that Gramps would enjoy discussing. 'Could a person dive from up there, Gramps?'

'It's possible, but hitting that water would be like hitting solid concrete.'

28

Dietmar grinned. 'Give it a try, Tom.'

Tom studied the bridge's support columns. 'It looks like a person could climb right up to the deck, using those ladders built into the columns. What do you think, Gramps?'

'I suppose so, but it would be instant death if you fell.'

'What a grim conversation,' Nanny said. 'Let's hurry along to the zoo, so we can see the monkeys.'

'Why bother, when we've got Dietmar?' Tom laughed, then turned to watch a big white ship heading out of the harbour. Its whistle blew for the bridge, and glistening waves curled from the bow as it steamed past.

'That's the *Princess of Vancouver*,' Nanny said. 'It's just left Pier A-3, heading for Nanaimo.'

'Pier A-3?' Tom said. 'But, that's . . .'

'That's what?'

'Oh, nothing,' Tom said, not wanting to worry Nanny and Gramps about his plan to investigate the pier for clues. 'Where's the zoo, Nanny?'

'Just past Lumbermen's Arch,' she said, pointing at a structure made of giant cedar logs. Several people stood near the arch, staring at a man with his hands in his pockets.

A brown squirrel was also watching the man. Whiskers twitching, it moved cautiously forward, then suddenly raced up the man's trouser leg, grabbed a peanut from his pocket and dashed away.

The onlookers applauded, and the man bowed. Wishing he had some peanuts to try the trick, Tom walked on with his grandparents to see the zoo's polar bears.

Instead of acting fierce they were asleep in the hot sunshine, pink tongues hanging out. A crowd of people ringed their grotto, hoping for action, but only saw one

29

bear raise a big head, look round grumpily, and go back to sleep.

'He could be Inspector Mort in disguise,' Tom said, laughing, 'especially when you read that sign!' He pointed to a warning notice, which read: *Polar bears have unpredictable tempers and are considered to be dangerous.*

'Now Tom,' Gramps said, trying to hide his smile, 'be polite.'

Nanny opened her purse. 'Here's some money for a snack,' she said. 'We'll meet you later at the Dining Pavilion.'

'OK, Nanny,' Tom said, 'and thanks for the treat!'

A sign pointing to a sea-lion tank tempted the boys, but they decided to eat first, and hurried along a path through the trees.

'What has four wheels and flies?' Tom asked.

'I don't know. Some sort of plane?'

'A garbage truck.' Tom laughed, then pointed to a parking lot beside the Dining Pavilion. 'Look!'

'What?' Dietmar asked, puzzled.

'That may be a dead person!' Tom said in excitement, indicating a Volkswagen with two feet sticking out of an open door. Then the feet shifted and a man sat up, rubbing sleepy eyes.

Dietmar laughed. 'The great detective strikes again!'

'Oh well,' Tom said, 'you can't win them all.' He led the way into the Dining Pavilion, and they went to sit at a table. Shortly after a waitress had taken their orders, some teenagers came in with Harrison Walsh.

The blond man waved at Tom as he sat down with the teenagers. Tom was studying their thin faces and dull clothes when the waitress put down two orange floats and handed Tom a slip of paper.

'Your bill, sir,' she said.

'No, I'm not. I'm Tom.'

The woman smiled briefly, then took Tom's money to a cash register. When she had gone, Tom leaned towards Dietmar. 'She's a drug addict,' he whispered out of the corner of his mouth.

'Why?'

'Look at her right arm.' Blue streaks marked the inside of the woman's arm below her elbow. 'Those are called tracks. All addicts have them.'

Dietmar's eyes narrowed, and he studied the woman as she returned with Tom's change. Then he laughed.

'What's the joke?' the woman asked.

'Nothing,' Dietmar said, laughing again. 'It's just this weird kid I'm with.'

The woman turned puzzled eyes to Tom before giving him his change and walking away.

'What's going on?' Tom whispered angrily. 'She looked at me like I had two heads.'

'Yeah,' Dietmar said, chuckling, 'and only half a brain. Those marks were made by that pen in her pocket.'

'What?'

Sticking out of a pocket at the woman's side was an order pad and a pen with a point that touched against her bare arm.

Trying to ignore Dietmar's chuckles, Tom leaned over his float. As he sucked creamy orange pop through his straws, he wondered if he dared tell Dietmar his theory about Harrison Walsh. He shouldn't discuss secret police matters, but he had to regain his reputation as a detective after looking like a fool with his theories about both the man in the Volkswagen and the waitress.

'All right, Dietmar,' he said, 'I've decided to tell you

something, but you must swear yourself to secrecy.'

'Is it worth it?'

'You bet.'

'OK,' Dietmar said, crossing his heart. 'I swear.'

'You see that blond man?'

'Yeah.'

'He is not what he seems,' Tom said, allowing himself to sound mysterious. 'I met him recently and he claimed to be a youth worker, but that was a lie.'

Dietmar shook his head. 'Is this your big secret?' he said scornfully.

Tom shielded his mouth with a hand. 'In actual fact,' he muttered, 'that man is an undercover police officer.'

For a moment Dietmar looked interested, then the scorn returned to his face. 'This sounds like another phoney theory, Austen. How do you know he's a cop?'

'Elementary, my dear Dietmar.' Tom enjoyed a drink, knowing he had Dietmar curious. 'First of all, I met him at the Police Club. Would the club admit someone who is not a police officer?'

'You were let in.'

Tom hesitated, realizing his theory wasn't perfect. 'Well, that's true,' he said, 'but I was told that man changed from police work to youth work so he could get more money. Everyone knows police officers are better paid.'

'Is that all the proof you've got?' Dietmar leaned over the straws in his empty glass and made a loud sucking noise. The waitress turned their way, looking annoyed, and Dietmar pointed at Tom. 'It was him!'

Tom gave Dietmar a sharp poke with his elbow. When the waitress looked away, he continued with his theory. 'I figure that man is only pretending to help teenagers with a drug problem. In fact, his police assignment is to get inside information about the Vancouver drug trade.'

Dietmar had lost interest in Tom's theory. When the waitress was busy, he swallowed several large gulps of air and released a loud belch, then jumped up and headed for the door, grinning.

Trying to calm the angry waitress with a smile, Tom slipped off his chair and backed towards the door. 'Sorry,' he said, feeling foolish, 'sorry.'

Going through the door, Tom glanced towards the corner; Harrison gave him a friendly smile, but Tom was still afraid that he had lost the big man's respect. Outside, brooding, he decided the best way to return to favour in Harrison's eyes would be to find some valuable clues at Pier A-3.

Tom decided to go there the very next morning, and immediately felt better. There was nothing like a good mystery to brighten his mood.

4

Tom climbed down a rocky slope to the water, then reached for an object under the oily surface. 'It's a boot!' he called to Dietmar, lifting it out of the sea.

'Big deal,' said Dietmar from the top of the slope.

Tom studied the rotting leather of the boot. 'There may be something in this.'

Dietmar laughed. 'I hope it's not a foot!'

Tom turned the boot over, thinking he might discover that it had belonged to the dead police agent, then tossed it back into the sea. After wiping his slimy fingers, he climbed up the slope and looked at Pier A-3.

'Nothing,' he said unhappily. 'An hour's search, and not a single clue.'

'Try the Yellow Pages,' Dietmar said, grinning.

Tom studied the harbour, wondering if he should forget the dead agent and concentrate on finding the drug smugglers for Inspector Mort. 'I already know how the smugglers operate,' he said, hoping to impress Dietmar. 'They use an underwater sea scooter to bring the drugs ashore from freighters.'

'That's possible,' Dietmar admitted. 'I saw a TV show where a sea scooter was used for smuggling.'

Pleased by Dietmar's reaction, Tom decided to think more seriously about the scooter, which had only been an idle guess. He watched a seagull swoop down to the water and come up with a wriggling fish, then looked along the shore towards a large hotel.

'There's the Bayshore Inn,' he said, pointing. 'That's where a friend of mine lives in a houseboat. Want to go and see it?'

'OK, but let's make it fast. My uncle is taking me camping for a couple of days, and we leave this afternoon.'

Tom nodded, then noticed a rusty circle of metal and bent to pick it up. 'Maybe this is a Shuriken,' he said, remembering the Oriental weapon that Bud had displayed in the Police Club. 'It could be a clue!'

'Not a chance,' Dietmar said. 'It's just an old gear from a car.'

'I guess you're right,' Tom said, throwing the object into the sea. For a moment he wondered if he'd just made a mistake, then shrugged and took out some Dubble Bubble. Passing a piece to Dietmar, he pointed to one of the office towers which stood along the waterfront. 'Did you hear about the two crazies who jumped off that building?'

'What happened?'

'Half-way down, one guy turned to the other and yelled: "So far, so good." '

Dietmar blew a large pink bubble. 'You should be on TV with your jokes.'

'Really?' Tom said happily.

'Yeah, then I could switch you off.'

Tom refrained from further joking, and they walked in silence to the houseboats. Going out on a wooden dock, which creaked with the movement of the sea, Tom and Dietmar gazed in surprise at the size of the luxurious houseboats.

'These places must cost a fortune,' said Tom, walking over to a big window. 'Look at the expensive furniture, and the panelled walls.'

'I always thought houseboats were dumps.'

'Me too,' Tom said. 'Harrison called his a little shack.'

Dietmar looked the length of the dock. 'There's no shacks here. That guy must live somewhere else.'

Tom shook his head. 'He said near the Bayshore Inn.'

'Look at the canary,' said Dietmar, pointing at a yellow bird which was fluttering desperately against a houseboat's window, trying to get out. On the dock nearby, a marmalade-coloured cat watched the bird closely, tail flicking.

'That poor canary,' Tom said. 'I wish I could help it.'

'Stick to not finding imaginary smugglers,' Dietmar said sarcastically, then glanced at his watch. 'I'm going home.'

Stung by Dietmar's comment, Tom tried to think of a new approach to his investigation. Pier A-3 had been a failure, but there was always the so-called club where the Scratcher had been given cover by the unfriendly man with the cigar. Deciding to try a stake-out the next day, Tom cheered up.

'Too bad about that boring camping trip,' he said. 'You're going to miss all the excitement.'

Dietmar laughed. 'Excitement? That'll be the day.'

The sky was cold and grey as Tom entered a patch of grass and trees called Victory Square, and selected a bench with a perfect view of the dark passage leading to the Scratcher's club.

On nearby benches Skid Road inhabitants nodded in sleep, or drank from bottles hidden in paper bags. Pigeons slept on the grass; close to them lay a man who had covered his body with newspapers as protection against the cold air.

Tom was too nervous to make notes, so he decided to memorize everything. He studied an approaching man in a wrinkled suit, then realized uneasily that he planned to share his bench.

'Down on your luck?' the man said, looking at Tom through glasses with dirt-speckled lenses.

Tom hadn't thought to prepare a cover story. 'Uh, no,' he stammered, 'I guess my luck's OK.'

The man sat down with a tired sigh. 'Go back to your mother and father, young man. No matter how tough things seem, running away is no solution.'

'I didn't run away.'

The man shook his head. 'You look kind of ragged to me.' Lifting his glasses on to his forehead, he settled down for a snooze.

Tom smiled, realizing he now blended into Skid Road. He was wearing ripped jeans, a frayed shirt and scruffy old shoes; earlier today, he'd combed some dirt into his hair before creeping out of the house without being spotted by his grandparents.

A bug with quivering feelers landed on Tom's arm. He watched it for a moment, then carefully studied the dark passage leading to the Scratcher's club.

As time passed, various seedy-looking people emerged from the passage, but there was no sign of the Scratcher or anyone suspicious enough to follow. The day grew colder, and Tom became depressed as he sat shivering in his old clothes; finally, in desperation, he decided to follow the next person who came out of the club.

This proved to be a strange-looking woman with hair cut so short that she looked almost bald. Staring around with large, liquid eyes that reminded Tom of Minnie Mouse, she turned east down Hastings Street.

Action at last! Tom hurried after Minnie, and within minutes had followed her into a department store, where she paused to study some expensive cameras.

Two sales clerks narrowed their eyes and moved closer, apparently expecting a major crime. Tom was also convinced Minnie looked like a crook, but he couldn't find a logical criminal pattern as she moved on through the store.

At last Minnie reached the book department, selected some poetry, and began to read from page one. Tom was tempted to check out the store's collection of Hardy Boys titles, but Minnie might then slip away from his surveillance.

'No! No!'

Tom's head snapped round towards the nearby cries, and he rushed to see the excitement. A teenage boy lay on the floor, holding up his arms in self-protection; close by, a man struggled to hold back a second boy.

'Nobody double-crosses me!' shouted the boy, whose high cheekbones gave him the appearance of a wolf.

'No!' The boy on the floor crawled backward, fear on his face. 'Don't hurt me!'

Suddenly, the wolf-boy wrenched free of the man and pulled out a knife. A silver blade flicked into view, but the man lunged forward and knocked the knife out of the boy's hand. It hit the floor, bounced, and landed at Tom's feet.

Quickly he picked up the knife to fling it away and prevent a stabbing. As he stared at the deadly blade, he heard running feet and someone grabbed his arm.

'Don't move,' a woman's voice said. 'I'm a store detective.'

Tom looked up at the woman, whose eyes were like steel. 'Give me your knife,' she ordered.

'It's not mine,' Tom said, his voice a whisper. With a trembling hand, he gave it to her.

Still gripping Tom, the woman opened a handbag which hung from her shoulder and reached inside. A radio microphone appeared on the end of a black cord which curled out of her handbag.

'Emergency,' she said. 'I need police assistance.'

Tom panicked. With terrible intensity, the fearful memory of being locked in the police cells flashed across his mind; he stared at the woman, then drove his foot down hard on her toes.

Pain crossed the woman's face, and her grip loosened. Tom pulled free and ran. The man reached to grab him but was knocked off balance by the wolf-boy. Tom headed through a nearby door and along the street, gasping for air as he ran. Slowing down for a red traffic light, he felt a hand touch his shoulder and turned to see the wolf-boy.

'This way,' he said.

Too frightened to think, Tom ran behind the boy across a parking lot and into a lane, where they stopped.

'You're a quick thinker,' the boy said, breathing hard.

39

'Stomping on that store detective created the confusion I needed to get free.'

'But what was the fight about?'

'I spotted that double-crosser in the store. I don't like people who cause me trouble.'

'Were you going to kill him?'

The wolf-boy smiled. 'I've got a bad temper. Say, kid, what's your name?'

'Tom Austen.'

'Call me Spider.' The boy studied Tom's old clothes, then shook his head. 'Another runaway, eh? Listen, Tom, I owe you a big favour for your help.'

Tom hardly heard the words. His mind had returned to the store, where at this very moment the woman was probably telling the police about him. 'I've got to go back, and tell them I wasn't involved.'

Spider laughed. 'You think they'd believe a runaway?'

'I don't know,' Tom admitted.

'Nobody knows who you were, so they'll file a report and forget the whole thing. Nobody got hurt, remember, and none of the store's precious stuff got ripped off.'

'Well, I guess that's true.'

Spider studied Tom, a smile at the corners of his mouth. 'I like your style, Tom. I could use someone like you.'

'I don't understand.'

Spider looked down the lane, which was deserted except for someone unloading cartons from a delivery van. Putting his arm around Tom's shoulders, Spider led him away from the van.

'You need money, right?' Spider looked carefully at Tom. 'Are you interested in working for me?'

Tom hesitated, uncertain what Spider was talking

about. It was hard to concentrate, with his mind still upset by events in the store.

'I need a courier, Tom, someone to deliver packages for me.'

'Packages?'

'Some people say they contain happiness.'

'You mean drugs?'

Spider nodded. 'You interested?'

'I don't think so,' said Tom, staring at Spider. With his high cheekbones, narrow eyes and black hair he looked dangerous, and there was even something frightening about the dark T-shirt and jeans he was wearing. 'I've never done anything like that.'

Spider smiled. 'Look, Tom,' he said in a friendly voice, 'you're new to the runaway scene, right? What are you going to do for money?'

'I'm not sure, but . . .'

Spider held up his hand. 'Tell you what. I'll describe my plan, then you can decide to either stay with me or split. How can you lose?'

'Well, that might be OK.'

'Good man. Let's go to Oppenheimer Park, then you can decide.'

Tom felt scared, torn between his fear of Spider and the realization that he had come across a person who was directly involved in the Vancouver drug trade. If he was brave enough to stay with Spider, he could dig out information that would be of real value to the police. But was he taking a foolish chance?

5

Two teams of kids were playing baseball in Oppenheimer Park; Spider and Tom went to sit under some
trees away from the action.

'I'm in this business to make money,' Spider said, 'but
I need your help to get more.'

'How?'

'First of all, I still have to check this idea with my
boss, but I can't see any objections. I spend my time
running round, collecting drugs from my boss and then
selling them to other people, and it's time I had some
help.'

Spider paused, thinking about his plan.

'I think we should hire you to sell dope to kids like

those ones playing baseball. Later, we'll recruit more sellers, and make ourselves a fortune.'

'But isn't that dangerous, when it's against the law?'

Spider flashed his friendly smile. 'We've already got a big business going, and we've never been caught. We'll protect you, Tom, and teach you survival tricks. What do you say?'

'I'm not sure.' Tom looked across the park to the baseball game, where a batter swung hard and sent the ball sailing in their direction. A curly-haired outfielder pursued the ball, then hurled it towards the catcher, but not in time to prevent a home run. Tom felt depressed, because the outfielder looked too young to be buying Spider's drugs.

'I'm supposed to sell to kids like that outfielder?'

'That's right,' Spider said in excitement. 'This is a great idea! All you do is hang around this park, getting to know the kids and passing out free samples of our drugs. After a while, the kids will get used to having them, and then you start charging money. It's as easy as falling off a log.'

'Aren't those kids kind of young?'

Spider shrugged. 'Only the weaklings will take your stuff, Tom, so we might as well get to them first. I never use dope, and I have no pity for anyone who does. I'm just selling a product, like a liquor store sells booze.'

Tom started to say that liquor stores don't sell to kids, then decided to remain silent. If he said too much, Spider might lose interest before Tom could get enough information to put Spider and his boss behind bars.

Managing a smile, Tom looked at Spider's narrow eyes. 'So, when do I start?'

Spider grinned. 'Good man! All right, I'm meeting

my boss in an hour, and I'll tell him my plan. Meanwhile, let's get you something to eat.'

Spider stood up with a wide smile, obviously delighted with the money he expected to result from his plan. As they left the park, the grey clouds released a few raindrops, warning the city to prepare for a soaking. Tom shivered, wishing he was anywhere but with Spider.

After the warning the rain came down in earnest, the fat little drops splattering against Tom and Spider. They hurried along the street, passing a woman who held a newspaper over her head, and finally found shelter in a doorway.

Turning his back to the wind, Spider rolled a cigarette. While he did this, Tom stared unhappily at the passing people, thinking he should have stayed home to drink hot chocolate and read a good mystery.

A teenage girl was coming their way, her straight black hair plastered against her head, rain rolling down her pudgy face and dripping from her chin. Her nose was red from the cold, and make-up from her eyes streaked her face like black tears. To Tom's surprise, she smiled in his direction.

'Well, hi!' she said, stopping at the doorway.

'Hi,' Tom said uncertainly.

Spider turned from lighting his cigarette, and looked at the girl. 'Hi there, ZZ.'

The girl smiled. 'It's good to see you.'

Spider inhaled some smoke, and glanced towards Tom. 'This is Tom Austen.'

The girl smiled briefly at Tom, then returned her eyes to Spider's face, her feelings about him so obvious that Tom felt embarrassed. When nothing more was said, he made room in the doorway for the girl. 'Why don't you get out of the rain?'

'OK, if nobody minds.' The girl blushed as she stepped closer to Spider and put down her shopping bag. Tom looked at her green eye-shadow and imitation-silver ear-rings, then at her brown coat, which he didn't think was real leather, all the while wondering if he should think of some conversation.

Instead, ZZ made a try. 'What weather!' she said, shaking some rain from her head. 'I hope you didn't get wet, Spider.'

'No,' he said, glancing down at his soaked T-shirt, 'I just stepped out of the bath-tub.'

Tom felt sorry for the girl, who smiled bravely. 'I'm not used to Vancouver rain,' he said. 'I've just arrived in town.'

Spider flicked away his cigarette and it landed, hissing, in a puddle. 'I've got an idea,' he said to the girl. 'How about fixing up a meal for Tom?'

'Sure!' she said, delighted to be of value. 'Are you coming too, Spider?'

'No, but I'll see you both later.'

Stepping into the rain, Spider walked quickly away. Tom waited until he had turned a corner, and ZZ could no longer stare after him, then he smiled. 'Well, I sure am hungry!'

ZZ's cheerfulness had disappeared with Spider, leaving her eyes empty. But then she shook her head, and smiled at Tom. 'Are you a friend of Spider's?'

'Sort of, I guess.'

'Ever been to Chinatown?'

'Nope.'

'Then come on,' ZZ said, returning to the storm. Taking a deep breath, Tom left the doorway and felt the cold rain lash his skin. Wiser people passed by safely under umbrellas, but Tom quickly became a sodden mess.

45

Fortunately, Chinatown was not far off, and Tom cheered up when they turned into Pender Street and ZZ stopped under a wide awning to inspect green vegetables displayed on wooden crates. Above each vegetable, a sign gave its name in Chinese and English.

'I love Chinatown,' said ZZ, smiling at Tom. 'I wish Spider would come with me, but he's not interested.'

'Are you his girlfriend?'

ZZ blushed, her face happy. 'Is that what you think?'

'Well, I don't know. I just wondered.'

'I wish he was my boyfriend.' ZZ looked sad for a moment, then smiled. 'I think he will be, one day.'

'Why?'

'I can just tell.' ZZ selected a lettuce and went inside the store to pay. Tom waited under the awning, watching the shoppers who crowded the street, most of them speaking Chinese. Even though he was wet and cold, Tom was glad he'd discovered this area.

'Hi,' ZZ said, appearing at Tom's side. 'Want to see something unusual?'

'Sure.'

ZZ led the way into a busy store, and along crowded aisles to a display case. 'Look at those!'

Tom saw a pile of snake skins; each skin was bent in a circle, head and tail tied together with three orange ribbons. 'What are they for?'

'I don't know. I'm too scared to ask.'

Tom saw a man working behind the display case. 'Excuse me, sir. What are the snake skins for?'

'They're used in ancient cures for disease,' the man said, smiling. 'That's what the toad skins are for, too.'

Next to the snakes was a stack of flattened toads, their arms and legs spread wide. Tom studied them, wishing he had one to slip into Dietmar's lunch at school.

'What a place!' he said to ZZ. 'I'm having fun.'

'Maybe you can get Spider to come next time.'

They left the shop, happy to see the rain had changed to a light drizzle. As they walked on, ZZ looked at Tom. 'How come you're Spider's friend?'

Tom felt uncomfortable, not knowing if ZZ was involved with Spider's operation. He hesitated, then decided that telling the truth would reduce the chances of getting into a mess. 'I've only just met Spider.'

'I've known him since I came to Vancouver.'

'Are you a runaway?'

'No.'

'Do you have a job?'

ZZ nodded. 'I work for a janitor company. Every night we go into those big high-rise buildings and clean the offices. I used to work in a laundry, but that wasn't much fun.'

Passing a tiny café, Tom stopped to stare in the window at a man who was using both hands to eat a bowl of soup. With his left hand he was spooning up some brown liquid while, with his right hand, he used chopsticks to lift skinny noodles and other objects out of the bowl. All the while, the man's eyes never left the copy of *Racing News* he was reading.

'What's that he's eating?' Tom asked.

'It's called Won Ton Soup.'

Tom grinned. 'That sounds pretty heavy.'

Unfortunately, the joke fell flat. ZZ thought about it for a moment, then they continued on their way. As they walked, Tom glanced at the streaks of make-up on ZZ's pudgy cheeks.

'Why are you called ZZ?'

'I don't know, actually. My real name is Joan, but Spider started calling me ZZ.'

47

Tom wondered how closely he should question ZZ about Spider's activities. It was a risk, but she might prove valuable. 'I guess Spider makes a lot of money, eh?'

ZZ smiled. 'I don't know, but for sure that's all he thinks about. Once he talked about having a family, but usually it's money, money, money.'

'How does he earn his living?'

ZZ frowned. 'He told me he imports stuff, but I think he was just kidding me.'

Tom felt a tickle of excitement. 'Did he say he imports it from the Orient?'

'No, he didn't say.'

Tom paused at a shop window, pretending to study its contents while he thought about Spider; if he was importing drugs from the Orient it would tie him directly to the police's smuggling investigation. The next important step was to learn the identity of Spider's boss.

'Who does Spider work for?' Tom asked, trying to sound casual.

ZZ lifted her shoulders in a shrug. 'Spider doesn't talk to me much, Tom.'

'Oh.'

Was ZZ's apparent lack of knowledge actually a clever cover for Spider? If so, Tom realized, he had better ease up on his questions or he might end up dropped in the harbour wearing a concrete overcoat.

Trying to change the subject, Tom gazed into the shop window. 'Look at that junk,' he said.

'This store's stuff is very nice,' ZZ said, looking around nervously to see if anyone had overheard Tom's rude remark.

Tom smiled. 'I meant that Chinese junk,' he said, pointing to a wooden model with elaborate sails.

'Oh, I see.' ZZ turned from the window. 'Come on, Tom, I want to show you *The Chinese Times* before we leave Chinatown.'

At the next corner, several people stood outside some office windows where the pages of a newspaper had been pinned up. Tom studied a headline, trying to figure out the intricate Chinese characters, then felt ZZ grab his arm. 'Look! That man just collapsed.'

Down a side street, Tom saw an old man in black clothes lying on his back; he struggled to raise his head, but was unable to lift it from the cold cement. A passing man looked uncomfortably at him, then walked quickly away.

'Hold this,' ZZ said, pushing her shopping bag into Tom's hand. Running to the man, she covered him with her coat. He looked at ZZ, trying to speak, then sighed.

A few people gathered, watching as ZZ gently brushed the man's white hair away from his face, speaking to him in a comforting tone. Tom heard the whoop-whoop-whoop of a siren and saw an ambulance swing round the corner, then pull to a stop. An attendant came to kneel beside ZZ.

'Thanks for your help,' he said. After an examination, the old man was lifted on to a stretcher and carried to the ambulance.

ZZ put on her coat and they started walking, listening to the ambulance's siren fading away into the other city sounds.

'I'm glad you were there,' Tom said. 'I didn't know what to do.'

'I hope he'll be OK.' They turned a corner, and ZZ smiled. 'We're almost home.'

As they approached ZZ's street, Tom noticed it was called Shanghai Alley and felt a flurry of fear when he saw the drab buildings that stood waiting.

6

'Surely you don't live here,' Tom said, staring at a ware-house with sagging grey walls.

'No.' ZZ laughed. 'I have a room in that hotel.'

Tom saw an old building with narrow windows and an iron fire escape. On the front of the hotel was a sign reading *Rooms by Week or Month.*

Tom felt a weight of fear and depression as they went inside. Immediately, he was hit by a sour smell, so strong that he was forced to put a hand over his face. Following ZZ up a flight of stairs, he had to struggle against the temptation to escape back outside into the fresh air.

They reached a hallway with a row of doors; the

nearest opened into a small office, where Tom saw a cardboard notice warning *No Visitors After 11 p.m.*, but there was no sign of a desk clerk.

Tom breathed as little sour air as possible while following ZZ to a door with a tin number 6 nailed to the wood. A woman came out of another door holding her stomach and walked shakily to the far end of the hallway, where the air was dark and gloomy except for a red *Exit* sign.

'Does that woman need help?' Tom asked.

'Molly?' ZZ shook her head. 'She just pretends to be sick to get attention. Later tonight she'll be drinking beer with a big smile on her face.'

Tom followed ZZ into her room, immediately grateful for the fresh air which flowed through the open windows. He pushed the door closed, first having to force it across the buckled linoleum on the floor, and looked around to see what ZZ called home.

Several posters of singers and movie stars had been put on the walls, but there was no way of overcoming the grim effect of the room. The brown bedspread had a number of holes from cigarette burns, and a wooden chair had also been scarred by cigarettes. Above a small table was an old mirror, in which Tom saw his bleak face reflected, and thin plastic curtains billowed at the windows.

Tom thought of his own room at home, and was unable to accept that ZZ lived like this. Footsteps crossed the ceiling above his head, then he heard the loud voice of a disc jockey as a radio was switched on. Again the feet walked over Tom's head, followed by the squeak of bed springs.

ZZ had gone into a small kitchen, and now returned with a packet. She scattered crumbs on the window sill;

within seconds there was the sound of wings, and a pigeon landed on the sill, its soft head bobbing as it went to work on the crumbs.

'They depend on me,' ZZ said. 'I feed them every day.'

Tom looked at ZZ's small collection of clothes, dangling from nails next to the glamorous faces of the stars on the posters, and felt a surge of pity for her lonely existence.

Sitting down on the scarred chair, he looked at ZZ. 'Why do you live here?'

'It's my home.'

'Couldn't you live somewhere else?' When ZZ didn't answer, Tom pressed the point. 'What about those apartment buildings near Stanley Park?'

ZZ laughed. 'I'm not rich, Tom.'

He was silent, staring at the pigeon as he thought about ZZ's predicament. 'Where do you come from?

'Radium Hot Springs.'

'Why don't you go back there? You could get a nice apartment in Radium Hot Springs, I bet.'

'I'm not going back, Tom. Vancouver is my home now.'

'Don't you get lonesome?'

ZZ shrugged, and reached into the packet for more crumbs. As she spread them on the sill Tom went to watch, but this frightened the pigeon and it flew away.

'Sorry,' said Tom.

'It'll come back,' ZZ said. 'Maybe I'm a bit lonely, but things will get better.'

'Well, I hope so.' Across a narrow space was another hotel, and Tom could see into several rooms where lights had been switched on as night came to the city. He looked down at a pigeon investigating an old piece of toast on the ground, then suddenly remembered his grandparents.

'Hey! I've got to make a phone call.'

'There's a phone beside the office. Want some money?'

Tom shook his head. He forced the door open over the linoleum, wondering how ZZ put up with this nuisance, and walked down the hallway, his nose wrinkled by the smell. Somewhere in the building, a radio played tinny music.

A young man with dirty blond hair sat in the office; he looked up with half-closed eyes at Tom, then appeared to nod back to sleep. Wishing he had some privacy, Tom called his grandparents' number.

'Hello, Gramps?' he said, when the phone was answered. 'This is Tom. Do you remember saying I could stay with Dietmar one night? Well, is it still OK?'

As Tom talked to his grandfather, he kept his eyes on the man in the office. Was he really dozing, or listening to the conversation?

'OK, Gramps,' Tom said at last. 'I'll be home tomorrow, and thanks a million.'

Tom hung up and started back to ZZ's room. He knew his grandparents wouldn't phone Dietmar's relatives to check his story, but betraying this trust made him feel terribly guilty. Tom could only hope that Nanny and Gramps would be forgiving when they learned he had helped put Spider behind bars.

When Tom opened ZZ's door, he was surprised to see a skinny teenage girl sitting on the bed. For a moment he couldn't place the girl, then remembered seeing her at the Shell station after his motorcycle ride with Harrison Walsh. Her long hair was still unwashed and greasy, and this time Tom noticed that her pale lips were marked

54

with sores. The girl was shivering in a thin blouse and worn jeans, her eyes staring at the floor. If she was coming to Spider for drugs, then Harrison's efforts to help the girl had been a failure so far.

'Hi,' Tom said. 'Remember me?'

The girl didn't answer. She rocked back and forth, trying to work up some warmth, then leaned against the wall.

ZZ came out of the kitchen. 'This is Angel,' she told Tom. 'I'm making her some soup while she waits for Spider.'

'Oh,' Tom studied the grey skin of Angel's face, then felt embarrassed when she looked up and caught him staring. He tried to smile, searching his head for conversation. 'Do you live here?' he asked brightly.

The girl returned her vacant eyes to the linoleum. Feeling foolish, Tom stayed beside the door, trying not to stare at Angel. He listened to the sound of the disc jockey describing his holiday in Hawaii, then smelled soup and went to the kitchen.

It was so small that Tom had to remain in the doorway, watching ZZ pour steaming soup into three bowls. He glanced at the tiny sink, and a cupboard holding a few dishes, then carried a bowl to Angel.

Reaching out silently, she put the bowl on her lap and warmed her hands over the steam rising from the dark red soup. Tom returned to the kitchen for his bowl, then sat on the wooden chair and began eating hungrily.

ZZ sat on the bed, but watched Angel instead of eating. Finally, she leaned forward. 'Eat your soup now, Angel,' she said quietly.

Angel rubbed the backs of her hands and blew on them before picking up her spoon. She lifted it to her mouth, but winced when the hot soup touched the raw sores on her lips. Putting down the spoon, she held her hands over the steam.

Tom glanced towards the windows, noticing that ZZ had closed them to keep Angel warm. The night was now dark, and he could see people moving about in the rooms of the other hotel. Briefly he wondered what was keeping Spider, then returned to his soup.

'This is good,' he said to ZZ.

'Thanks, Tom.'

The door was pushed open. Tom expected to see Spider, but instead it was a man wearing an old coat, blue trousers and scuffed white shoes. A worried smile on his face, the man took a cigarette out of his mouth. 'Where's Spider?'

'I don't know,' ZZ answered.

'There's a note on his door, saying to call at room 6. So where is he?'

'Spider always leaves that note,' ZZ said. 'I'm just supposed to tell people to wait, or take a message.'

The man inhaled some smoke, then coughed. After studying Tom, he left the room.

'What a rude person,' ZZ said.

'Ever seen him before?' When ZZ shook her head, Tom returned to his soup. 'Let's watch TV.'

'I don't have one.'

'What?' Tom said, surprised. 'How do you keep entertained?

ZZ glanced up at the ceiling. 'I've got my neighbour's radio. The disc jockeys are like personal friends.'

Angel handed her uneaten soup to ZZ. 'Tell Spider I've got to see him,' she said, going to the door. When she had trouble getting it open, Tom went to help.

'Good-bye,' he said, but there was no reply.

Feeling fresh air touch his back, Tom turned to see

ZZ opening the windows. With the fresh air came noises from the hotel rooms opposite. Tom heard voices, laughter, radios tuned to various stations, and someone clapping along to music.

'I guess I was wrong about you being lonely,' he said, smiling. 'There's lots of company.'

'I suppose so,' ZZ said. 'But Spider's callers aren't exactly the same as having friends.'

'ZZ, is there a washroom?'

'Sure, down at the end of the hallway.'

'Thanks.' Tom went out, expecting another caller to be in ZZ's room when he returned. Hurrying down the hallway to avoid the smell, he found a door marked *Toilet* and turned the handle. The door opened slightly, then seemed to jam against something. Tom pushed harder, and managed to get it wide enough to put his head inside.

The small room was in darkness, but dim light came from the hallway. The door was hitting against a dark bundle jammed between the toilet and the wall, and Tom reached down to push the bundle to one side. With a shock, he felt the warmth of a body.

As Tom's heart leapt, the bundle shifted slightly and the white smudge of a face rose from the floor. 'It's OK, friend,' a man's voice said, his words mixed with the smell of alcohol.

'Are you,' Tom said, having trouble speaking, 'are you sick?'

'No, friend,' the voice said. 'Let me sleep.'

The man's head dropped back to the floor, and Tom closed the door. His heart was pounding from shock, and he leaned his head against the wall while he tried to breathe.

Finally, going to open a door under the red light, Tom

saw a flight of stairs. Darkness settled around him as he started to feel his way upward.

It was a frightening experience, but Tom found his way to a washroom on the next floor. This one was empty, and even had a light, but Tom was still nervous as he went inside and turned the lock.

Trying not to notice the smell, Tom read the messages all over the walls. One person had written *Your ennemi is cop, juge, lawers,* and someone else had scrawled *PIGS no good PIGS PIGS,* but other people had been satisfied with contributing names, dates and drawings.

Tom reached to flush the toilet, then drew back his hand. How many germs waited invisibly on that handle? Covering his fingers with a piece of toilet paper, he pushed the handle and quickly left the washroom, wondering how someone as nice as ZZ could choose to live like this.

Opening ZZ's door, he was not surprised to see the chair occupied by another caller. Smiling at his cleverness in predicting this, Tom closed the door as the newest visitor turned his way.

'Hi,' said Tom, his smile disappearing when he saw the man's face. His nose was flat and his skin looked unhealthy, but it was the look in the man's cold eyes that really scared Tom.

'Who's this?' the man said, his voice rough in his throat.

'A friend of Spider's.' ZZ sat on the bed, fiddling nervously with the pillow.

'I've never seen him before.' The man lifted his hand and gestured at Tom. 'Come here. Let me have a look at you.'

Tom hesitated, then obeyed the command. Stepping closer, he tried not to show his fear as the man's unfriendly eyes examined his face, then dropped to Tom's old clothes. Reaching out a big hand, the man shoved Tom and he sprawled back on the bed.

'Stay there,' the man ordered, then turned to stare at the door.

Tom lay where he had fallen, afraid to move, his eyes fixed on the collar of the man's pink shirt, where sweat and dirt had formed a dark stain. Then the bed shifted as ZZ stood up.

'I'm going to make some tea,' she said.

'Sit down,' the man ordered, his eyes still on the door.

To Tom's surprise, he heard ZZ walk to the kitchen. He waited anxiously for the man to erupt in fury, but nothing happened. There was the sound of water running into a kettle, and the gentle cooing of a pigeon on the sill, but Tom didn't dare turn to look behind. Perhaps ZZ was secretly preparing a way to get rid of this evil man; if so, Tom hoped she would hurry.

ZZ came out of the kitchen and walked to the man with a steaming mug in her hand. 'Do you want sugar?' she asked, offering him the tea.

Standing up, the man slapped ZZ hard across the face. She was knocked sideways against the wall, the hot tea leaping from the mug and splashing across her jeans as she fell on the floor. For a second there was silence, then ZZ began to sob.

The man sat down. 'Next time you'll know to listen.'

Tom stared at ZZ, his mouth open in disbelief. She had been hit so quickly that he had been unable to react, and now he was afraid to do anything. Finally, as ZZ stopped crying, Tom found enough courage to speak.

'It'll be OK,' he told ZZ. 'When Spider gets here, he'll help us.'

She was silent, looking at the man with eyes red from

crying, and Tom felt humiliated that he was powerless to give her help or comfort. Everything was going wrong, and he felt more lost and lonely than ever before in his life.

A long time passed without anyone moving or speaking. Finally, to Tom's relief, he heard voices approaching in the hallway and realized one of the speakers was Spider.

'I'll see you tomorrow,' Spider's voice said. The handle rattled, and his wolf-like face appeared in the doorway.

'What's this?' he said, looking down at ZZ on the floor. Then, seeing the man, he smiled. 'Hi there, Leo. Been waiting long?'

'Too long,' the man replied.

'The boss told me you'd be calling for the money,' Spider said. 'Sorry I'm late.'

'You and me both. Where is it?'

Spider took out an envelope and handed it to the man. There was silence while he counted the envelope's contents, then nodded. 'I'll see you tonight at the yards,' he told Spider, and left the room.

'Spider!' Tom said, getting up quickly. 'Don't let him get away! He beat up ZZ.'

Spider glanced at ZZ's face, where the skin was swollen and red. 'What did you do?'

'I don't understand,' she said.

'You must have done something to get Leo angry.'

'No, she didn't!' Tom said. 'He hit her for no reason.'

Spider shrugged, and turned to leave. 'Let's go to my room, Tom. We've got some talking to do.'

'But what about that guy? Aren't you going to beat him up for hurting ZZ?'

Spider looked impatient. 'Leo and my boss are a

team, Tom. What Leo did to ZZ is no concern of mine.'

'But . . .'

'Are you coming with me? Or are you staying here?'

Tom watched Spider leave the room, then turned to ZZ. She had started to cry again, but managed a smile when Tom tried to speak. 'I'll be OK,' she said. 'Go on with Spider.'

'Can't I help?'

ZZ shook her head. 'Good luck, Tom.'

'Maybe I'll see you again.'

ZZ nodded. Tom left the room, feeling sad about ZZ. Spider was waiting under the red light, and Tom walked quickly his way, trying to concentrate on putting Spider behind bars. That would be perfect revenge for the way he had treated ZZ.

7

Spider lit a match to cut the darkness as they started up the stairs. 'Don't worry about ZZ. She gets upset too easily.'

'I like her.'

'She's OK,' Spider looked at Tom, the yellow light flickering on his face. 'People with soft hearts don't survive in this business.'

'I'm not soft.' Tom tightened the muscles around his mouth and eyes, trying to look tough. 'You can count on me, Spider.'

'I'm not so sure,' he said, studying Tom. The match went out; in the sudden darkness Tom felt an intense fear of Spider, and stepped back close to the wall.

Another match flashed into life. 'I'm going to give you a chance,' Spider said, 'but one mistake and you're finished.'

Reaching the next floor, they went to Spider's room. This time no refreshing air blew through the windows; the musty smell of dirty clothes was overpowering as Spider switched on a lamp.

The room was even more depressing than ZZ's. Spider had not tried to brighten his walls, and his bed was a jumble of blankets and sheets grey with dirt.

'Thirsty?' he asked.

'No thanks.' Tom looked at Spider's scattered clothes, then noticed the linoleum was so old that black paths had been worn into it by thousands of footsteps.

Spider pushed up a window, letting in the night noises. A wooden box stood outside on a small platform; he reached inside and took out a beer. Snapping off the lid, he tossed it into the darkness before closing the window.

Tom noticed there wasn't a kitchen. He wondered what Spider did for meals, then saw the crumpled remains of McDonald's hamburger containers beside the bed. It was hard to accept that he and Spider enjoyed the same food.

'Let's talk,' Spider said, dropping down on to the bed. 'I'm going to hire you.'

Not knowing if he should look pleased, or continue to display a tough face, Tom nodded. 'Good.'

'I'm finished with my boss.' Spider drank some beer, and looked carefully at Tom. 'What do you think of that?'

'I don't know,' Tom answered, uncertain what he was expected to say. 'What happened?'

Spider shook his head, looking angry. 'I started to

outline my plan, and the boss tore a strip off my hide. He said it was stupid to sell to kids; he said I was crazy. I could have killed him, but I played it smart.'

'How?'

'I kept my mouth shut, then left to have a beer and think about my plan. I've made a big decision, Tom. Later tonight I'm meeting my boss and Leo, and I'll tell them I quit. I'm going to set up my own territory, starting with those kids at Oppenheimer Park.'

'But won't they be angry?'

'Look, Tom, my boss turned down the chance to open up that new territory. It's my plan, and I'm going to use it to cash in.' Spider lifted his beer. 'I bet when I tell the boss more of my plans, and especially about this clever kid I've hired, he'll change his mind. But I'm finished with him, Tom.'

There was a knock, and Tom's heart jumped. Spider glanced towards the door, then casually finished his beer. 'Answer that.'

Tom went slowly to the door, afraid that Leo had returned. But it was ZZ who stepped nervously into the room and looked at Spider.

'I forgot to tell you,' she said. 'Angel came by, and said she had to see you.'

'OK,' Spider said. 'Any other messages?'

'No.' ZZ waited for Spider to speak, but he took out his tobacco and began to roll a cigarette. ZZ glanced at Tom with a small smile and left the room.

'Close the door.' Spider tipped some clothes off the chair, and motioned for Tom to sit down. 'One time I asked ZZ if she wanted a ring,' he said, smiling at the memory. 'When she said yes, I told her to get one out of the bath-tub.'

Tom felt like a traitor as he forced himself to laugh.

'I once told ZZ to get out of Vancouver, but she chose to stay.' Spider held out the cigarette, and looked thoughtfully at the glowing red tip. 'It always amazes me how people allow their lives to become a mess.'

'Yeah, I guess so.'

'People should be like me and my boss. Nothing gets in the way of our business.' Spider glanced at Tom. 'You know what I mean by a snake?'

'No.'

'OK, lesson number one for my new employee. A snake is an undercover informer for the police.'

'You mean a nark?'

Spider looked surprised, then grinned. 'Good man! You know more than I thought.'

For a moment Tom felt pleased, then realized he should actually be playing dumb. If he displayed any more knowledge of criminal expressions, Spider might become suspicious.

'Recently a snake got on to our operation,' Spider said. 'Leo and my boss arranged a meeting with him last Friday and he was snuffed, then dumped off Pier A-3.'

'You mean he was killed?' Tom said, too shaken to remember about playing dumb. 'Then he must have been . . .'

'Been who?' Spider said, looking surprised.

'Uh, no one,' Tom said, his face turning red. 'He, um, must have been a clever snake, but not clever enough.'

'You bet,' Spider said, leaning back and inhaling some smoke.

Tom stared at Spider, his nerves tingling. Surely the dead man was the police agent whose body had been found at Pier A-3, which meant that Leo and Spider's boss were guilty of both drug-dealing and murder. This alone was valuable information for the police, but they would also want to know the identity of Spider's boss. How could Tom discover it?

Spider smiled. 'Sometimes I don't understand my boss. He makes a lot of money out of this operation, so you'd think he would drive around town in the fanciest car possible. That's what I'll do, when I'm rich.'

'But, I mean, have kids got enough money to make you rich?'

'Sure, Tom. Once they're steady drug users, they'll steal money from home, or other kids at school, anywhere.' Spider smiled. 'The boss has some terrific stories about the things customers do to get money.'

He turned towards the window. 'It's going to be tough to set up my business without inside information from the boss about police plans.'

'What?' Tom said, startled.

'The boss has always protected our operation with confidential information from inside police head-quarters. Every time some new snakes move out, the boss has already warned me and Leo.'

Tom waited silently, not wanting to appear eager for information, while Spider stared into the hotel rooms opposite. 'Look at those poeple,' he said. 'What a way to spend your life.'

The room was quiet while Spider thought. 'There are some things we can do better than the boss. For example, we need a better place to hide our products.'

Tom glanced around, wondering if Spider was about to reveal a secret hiding place, but he continued to look out of the window.

'The boss keeps his stuff safely hidden in moisture-proof packages, which is OK.' Spider paused, thinking. 'But I really get nervous, when he's fumbling with his cap and I'm waiting for some cop to appear out of nowhere. It takes forever just to get my hands on the stuff.'

'I'm not sure what you mean,' Tom said, hoping for some details.

'We need a good place to carry our drugs. A hollow transistor radio may be the answer.'

There was a quiet knock at the door; without waiting for an order, Tom went to answer it. Angel stood in the hallway, hugging her thin body.

'I've got to see Spider.'

'That you, Angel?' Spider called.

'Yeah.'

Spider dropped his cigarette on the floor, crushed it under his heel, then went into the hallway and closed the door. Tom tried to hear their conversation, but they walked away.

Suddenly Tom felt terribly tired. There was nothing he wanted more than to go home, but now he was too involved in this case to back out. Going to the window, he looked out towards the city.

The neon lights were pretty, but they belonged to another world and gave Tom no comfort. Sighing, he gazed at the hotel rooms opposite, feeling that he was trapped in a terrible nightmare.

The smell of the room was suffocating. Although he knew Spider might get angry, Tom opened the window and leaned outside for some fresh air. Immediately he was assaulted by the noise from the other hotel windows, and gagged on the greasy smell of sausages being fried in a room somewhere below.

Tom noticed the box Spider used as a refrigerator. Did it hold anything other than beer? He felt around inside, but there was nothing.

He should search the room, but what if he was caught? Remembering a detective handbook that advised checking for articles taped under furniture, Tom went to the chair and turned it over, but found only wads of hardened gum.

Dropping to his knees, Tom looked under the bed. The floor was thick with dirt, cigarette butts, dust and bits of food; feeling nauseous, Tom crawled into this mess to study the bottom of the mattress.

Nothing. He slid out and stood, brushing off the dirt. Picking up a pair of Spider's jeans, he found a box of matches from a Vancouver restaurant. Keeping the matches, he worked his way through the rest of the clothes without finding anything else.

Tom's body was shaking. Spider could return at any moment, and there was still a closet to search. Was it worth the risk? He hesitated, picturing Spider bursting through the door with rage on his face.

From outside came the sound of a radio being tuned. 'This is your Information Station radio car,' an announcer said, 'broadcasting direct from the B.C. Penitentiary, where inmates have rioted and two guards are being held hostage . . .' There was a squeal, followed by half a sentence advertising Eagle Ford, then another squeal before the radio produced a song.

Tom went to the closet, then heard footsteps and turned his frightened face towards the door. The handle rattled, and he just managed to step back from the closet before Spider came into the room. 'Whatcha doing?' he asked.

'Nothing,' Tom said, his heart racing.

Spider glanced round the room, then went for a beer. Throwing the lid into the night, he studied Tom. 'You shouldn't have done that.'

'What?' Tom said, his eyes going wide in fear.

'Opened the window.' Spider drank some beer, and wiped his mouth with the back of his hand. 'You must always ask permission. That's how my boss treats me.'

'Sorry. I didn't think.'

His face disapproving, Spider looked out of the window. Tom quickly studied the scattered clothing, hoping he hadn't disturbed a special arrangement, then wondered what he should do next. If Spider was really going to quit, tonight would be Tom's only chance to get a look at his boss.

'May I go to your meeting?'

Spider shook his head. 'I'll do this alone. You get some sleep, and tomorrow we'll plan our operation.'

'When's the meeting?'

'Not for a couple of hours.' Spider carried the chair to the window and sat down. Propping his feet on the sill, he rolled a cigarette. 'I'm going to do some heavy thinking. You grab some shut-eye.'

'OK,' Tom said reluctantly, knowing he mustn't arouse Spider's suspicions. He would pretend to sleep, then secretly follow Spider to his meeting place.

Sitting down on the bed, he dropped his shoes on the floor. Mentally holding his nose, he lay down on the dirty sheets and put his head on the lumpy pillow. His scalp felt itchy and he had an unpleasant vision of lice crawling into his hair; sitting up quickly, he rested against the wall.

'What's that?' Spider said, looking down at the floor.

Tom expected to see a giant rat, but nothing was visible. 'What's what?'

'In your shoe.' Spider picked it up and took out the cash. 'Is this where you keep your money?'

Tom blushed, then felt scared. Did other snakes hide money in their shoes while working in Skid Road? 'I, uh, I couldn't afford a wallet,' he said nervously. 'Besides, I've got holes in my pockets.'

Spider studied Tom's face. What if he asked to see the pockets? But he smiled and dropped the money back inside Tom's shoe. 'You're crazy, kid, but I like you.'

'Thanks,' Tom said, relieved but still nervous. None of this would be happening, he thought, if only he was interested in a safe job, like cleaning office buildings. This made him wonder how ZZ was getting along in her lonely room.

'Why did you give ZZ that strange name?'

Spider smiled. 'A is the first letter in the alphabet, Z is the last. And ZZ is so useless, she rates a double Z.' Spider switched off the lamp, and the room became a confusing pattern of darkness, cut by lights from outside. Again Tom felt like a traitor, remembering ZZ's gentleness to the old man yet failing to say anything in her defence.

Spider sighed with contentment. 'ZZ reminds me of how I broke into crime.'

'Why?'

'When I was younger, I mugged a Brownie.' Spider chuckled as he sucked on his cigarette. 'She was a dumbie, like ZZ. Anyway, she'd been selling those Girl Guide cookies, and I got away with all her cash.'

Spider laughed happily, enjoying the memory. 'When I got that whiff of easy money, there was no stopping me.'

'Aren't you afraid of getting caught?'

'No way. Only fools get caught, and I'm no fool.'

Tom allowed himself a secret smile, knowing Spider would soon regret making that boast. From another room came the music of a harmonica, then it was interrupted by the sound of a breaking bottle. Someone swore loudly, another voice said 'ah sheddup', and the music resumed.

Tom's sleepy eyes were closing. Thinking water splashed on his face would keep him awake, he stood up. 'OK if I wash?'

Spider switched on the lamp. 'There's a towel around somewhere.'

Tom had seen it while searching Spider's clothes, but carefully took his time finding it. He went to the sink, and saw a large brown bug walking along the enamel. 'Ugh,' he said, staring at the bug.

'Kill it,' Spider ordered.

The bug stopped, almost as if it had understood Spider. Tom wished it would retreat to safety, but it seemed to think being motionless made it invisible.

Spider repeated his order, this time impatiently. Tom reached forward, but he couldn't bring himself to crush the bug and, instead, flicked it into the sink. Pretending he had lost interest in washing, he returned to the bed and lay down.

Spider rolled yet another cigarette, then switched off the lamp. Before the light went out, Tom noticed several cigarette burns on an uncovered corner of the mattress and realized what a death trap this hotel would be if someone fell asleep while smoking.

Sirens and the angry sound of car horns came out of the night, then there was a time of peace and Tom's mind began to drift.

He closed his eyes for one minute, just to rest them, and saw himself on a bright TV screen, playing the harmonica for a large audience. Then the picture changed, and Tom was inside the Information Station radio car, broadcasting a message to the anxious public that all was well and the hostages had been freed unharmed. Yes, all was well, and Tom slept.

71

8

'Get out of here!'

Tom sat up, looking into the confused darkness. Where was he? His mind struggled to make sense of smells, noises and a window which framed the night outside.

'Get out!' a woman shouted. 'You stay away for two days, then come back. I don't want you!'

The shouts were coming through the wall. At last, as a man's voice muttered apologies, Tom remembered. He had fallen asleep, and Spider had left for the meeting. Tom had failed.

He put on his shoes and went to the window, his heart heavy. Looking up at a display of brilliant stars, his spirits slowly revived.

The woman behind the wall was sobbing, a sad sound that made Tom think of ZZ. Perhaps she knew where Spider had gone. Suddenly hopeful, Tom crossed the room and stepped into the hallway's foul air.

Half-way to ZZ's room, he remembered that she worked nights. This was a blow to his spirits, but he continued on and knocked loudly on her door. It was his only chance.

Silence. Tom knocked again. He thought he heard bed springs, and leaned against the door to listen. There were footsteps, then the sound of the handle. Tom smiled in relief as the door scraped open and ZZ's sleepy face appeared.

'Tom?' she said, squinting.

'Please, ZZ, may I talk to you?' Tom waited for a reaction, but she only yawned and scratched her head.

'Please, ZZ, let me in.'

'Well, OK. Just for a minute.'

Tom entered her room, hearing laughter. He looked up at the ceiling, recognizing a comedian's voice on the neighbour's radio, then turned to ZZ. 'Why aren't you working?'

'It's my night off.' She tightened the cord of her dressing gown and sat down. 'What is it, Tom?'

'I need help.' He paused, wishing he'd decided beforehand how to approach ZZ. Probably he should tell the truth, but as little as possible. 'I need to find Spider right away.'

'Why?'

'He may be in danger,' he said, surprising himself with the answer. Of course there was a danger to Spider from Tom, but he also wondered suddenly how Leo and Spider's boss would react to him quitting.

'What danger?'

'I'm not sure yet, but I must find Spider. Do you know where he is?'

ZZ shook her head. 'I've been sleeping for hours, Tom.'

'Well, has he ever said where he meets his boss?'

ZZ looked out of the window, thinking. 'Is he really in danger?'

'Yes!'

'OK,' she said, making a decision. 'Last night Spider left instructions for a man to meet him in the railway yards off Carrall Street.'

'Would you come with me to those yards?'

'Why?'

'Because Spider may be in danger, I need to find him right away, and I don't know where Carrall Street is. Please, ZZ, help me!'

Perhaps moved by Tom's pleading, ZZ stood up. 'Wait outside while I dress.'

'Great!' said Tom, delighted. He went into the hallway and considered his plans. Soon he would have to contact the police, but first he must try to get a look at Spider's boss.

ZZ came out wearing her imitation-leather coat; she had put on ear-rings and make-up, and Tom wondered if this was for Spider's benefit.

'I hope Spider is safe,' she said anxiously.

Tom wanted to reassure ZZ, but soon she would have to know Spider was heading for prison. So he remained silent as they walked along the hallway, listening to the radios and voices that seemed never to stop.

Stepping out of the hotel was wonderful. Tom paused to breathe cold air deep into his lungs, hoping he would not have to return to the hotel for one hundred thousand years, then he started walking.

They were soon in the heart of Skid Road, and found it active even in the darkest hours of the night. Two men sat on a bench at a bus stop, drinking from a bottle hidden in a paper bag; nearby, a shabby figure searched a rubbish bin.

In the next block, an enormous truck roared out of a lane, almost hitting a bedraggled drunk. As it thundered away, leaving behind the stench of diesel fumes, Tom wondered how ZZ could be so blind to the ugliness of Skid Road.

'I wish you'd go home to Radium Hot Springs,' he said.

ZZ was silent, then pointed to the glow of street-lamps in the distance. 'There's Gastown.'

'Let's hurry!' Tom said, his depression lifting away as he recognized the clean beauty of Maple Tree Square. When they emerged from the darkness, Tom stopped to gaze at the green leaves and clusters of white street-lamps, thrilled to be back in a safe world.

'What about Spider?' ZZ asked, when Tom made no effort to move on.

'Oh, yeah,' he said, remembering unhappily that his investigation must continue. 'Where are those railway yards?'

'Over there,' ZZ answered. 'Just beyond the lights.'

After crossing the square, they returned to darkness. The depression that came with it was twice as powerful as before, and Tom had to struggle to keep from turning back.

A green signal light was visible ahead, and Tom heard the squeak and squeal of train wheels rolling slowly along steel rails, but he could make no sense of the dark shapes in the railway yards.

'Tom?' asked ZZ. 'Why does Spider have his meetings in such a strange place?'

'I'll tell you later.'

'I'm scared,' ZZ whispered after a moment.

'It'll be OK,' Tom said, hoping his own nervousness wasn't obvious. Slowly he walked forward, feeling cinders and gravel crunch under his feet, fear growing with every step. Where was Spider hiding?

'Tell me something,' Tom whispered. 'Where exactly did Spider meet that man?'

'He said to go to the *Carpetland* warehouse.'

Somewhere in the night a train started to move forward, causing a series of loud bangs to ripple down its length as each car yanked on the one behind. Hoping the noise would cover their crunching footsteps, Tom led the way towards a warehouse where a dim sign read *Carpetland*.

There was no trace of Spider. Tom squinted his eyes, hoping to spot the red glow of his cigarette, but saw only darkness.

'There!' said ZZ, grabbing Tom's arm and pointing. 'He must be in that shack.'

His heart pounding, Tom watched ZZ start towards a small shack near the warehouse wall. 'There may be a trap!' he warned, but ZZ kept on and Tom was forced to follow. He saw ZZ reach the shack, bend down in the doorway, then turn with a frightened face.

'It's Spider,' she said. 'He's badly hurt.'

Still fearing a trap, Tom went slowly forward. Spider lay face down on the floor of the shack, his breathing weak.

'Help me turn him over,' ZZ said. Tom knelt down to assist, and she gently rolled Spider on to his back, then wiped some dirt from his face. 'I'm going for help,' she said, standing up.

'Where?'

'The police station isn't far.' ZZ turned and ran, the sound of her feet dying away into the darkness.

Leaning towards Spider, Tom put his hands on the floor of the shack and felt a sharp pain. Looking down, he saw the floor was littered with cigarette and cigar butts, matches, and the splintered remains of a silver-coated lens. Tom pulled a glass sliver out of his hand, then bent forward as Spider moaned and opened his eyes.

'Who beat you, Spider? Was it your boss?'

Slowly, Spider shook his head. 'It was Leo,' he whispered painfully.

'Why? Because you wanted your own territory?'

Spider nodded, then looked at Tom with hatred. 'You lousy punk,' he whispered. 'You're a police informer, not a runaway.'

'What?'

'I described you to my boss, and he knows you.'

Gripped by horror, Tom stared at Spider.

'Leo and my boss are after you. Say your prayers, boy.'

'But how could he know me?' Tom said, unwilling to believe it was possible. Surely Spider was lying, but why? 'Who is your boss, Spider? Please, tell me his name.'

The fear in Tom's voice made Spider smile, and then he closed his eyes. Tom stood up, and turned to stare into the dark night. For several minutes he thought desperately about Spider's frightening statement, then he heard the sound of an approaching siren.

The siren should have represented safety to Tom, but before the police could arrive he turned and ran quickly into the darkness.

9

Later the same night Tom stood beside a stone wall, staring at a sheltered cove. To his left, thick trees formed a dark curtain across the entrance to Stanley Park.

Tom looked up at the silver circle of the moon, where astronauts had left their footprints, and wondered if standing in that desolation was as lonely as standing by a stone wall, afraid to turn back and afraid to go forward.

Lifting his cold hands, Tom blew on his fingers. In the east, a red smudge had appeared low on the horizon, the first warning that the dawn was coming. He must move on.

Turning, he moved towards the park. Across a nearby road was Lost Lagoon, where spotlights shone on jets of water which rose from a fountain. The road which ran through the park to Lions Gate Bridge was blocked off by signs reading *Bridge Closed for Resurfacing*.

As Tom walked nervously through the gloomy park, a bird with a squeaky voice called from the branches above. The trees grew all around, shutting out the lights of the city and reaching high above his head to hide the stars. But he was not alone, for loud squawks and cries came out of the darkness, drawing Tom forward towards the zoo.

He passed a silent playground, the swings empty of life. Shivering, Tom hurried on towards the loud cries, thankful when the dim shapes of the zoo cages appeared ahead.

He spotted the phone booth he remembered from his last visit, and hurried over. He got out a piece of paper, called a number, then waited a long time before it was answered. 'Hello, Harrison?' he said at last. 'I'm sorry to disturb you, but I need help badly.'

Tom gave Harrison brief details of his predicament, and arranged a meeting. He then called Bud, the officer he had met in the Police Club, but he was out on patrol duty. After giving an urgent message to Bud's wife, Tom hurried on his way.

Leaving the zoo behind, he came to Lumbermen's Arch, where he had last seen a man feeding peanuts to a squirrel. Now a low white mist lay across the grass, beyond it a narrow strip of the sea and the mountains of North Vancouver.

The smell of sea air reminded Tom of his mission, and he forced himself to move on. Reaching the sea wall, the full length of Lions Gate Bridge was visible ahead, red lights shining from its tall support columns.

Powerful currents at the mouth of the harbour made the sea rough as Tom approached the bridge. Heavy waves rushed in, swirling among the boulders where seagulls rested; the intensity of the sea was frightening, and Tom was glad to spot the path which led up the side of the nearby bluff.

Leaving the sea wall, he started up the steep path. Branches reached to touch his face, and he slipped on pebbles and small rocks, but at last he reached the top.

Puffing from his climb, Tom walked to the empty road which came out of the park and led on to the bridge. Although the resurfacing equipment waited beside the road, there was no sign of the work crew at this hour. Two lions guarded the approach, but they were carved from stone and stared silently into the dark shadows of the park.

Thinking about the problems he still faced, Tom walked slowly out on to the bridge to the first support column. Glancing down, he was shocked to see the water so far below.

Quickly lifting his eyes, Tom looked at the eastern sky, where the colours reflected from thin clouds suggested that the sun would arrive at any minute. Briefly Tom was distracted, glancing towards Stanley Park when he heard a motorcycle, then looked east just as the sun appeared. Squinting, he looked at the orange path it made across the harbour, then again looked towards the park.

A motorcycle had paused in the dark shadows, but now picked up speed and roared out on to the bridge. The boom of the big Harley-Davidson's engine disturbed the quiet dawn as Harrison Walsh rushed towards Tom and pulled to a stop.

'Thanks for coming!' Tom said happily. 'I really need help.'

Harrison took off his helmet, his blond hair and beard lit by the early morning sunshine. 'Let's hear your story in detail, Tom.'

Carefully, Tom described his undercover investigation, starting with the stake out at Victory Square and ending with the events in the railway yards. Had all that happened in such a short time? It was difficult to believe, just as Tom could hardly accept that Skid Road really existed when he looked beyond Stanley Park to the peaceful city.

'There's one thing I don't understand,' Harrison said. 'Why a meeting on this bridge?'

'Because I need your help against Spider's boss.'

'You know his identity?' Harrison asked, surprised. 'Who is it?'

'Inspector Mort.'

Tom had expected a startled gasp from Harrison, but the big man only smiled and shook his head. 'A police inspector?' he said. 'I doubt it, Tom, but why do you think so?'

'Spider told me his boss gets confidential information from inside police headquarters,' Tom answered. 'The Inspector could easily do that.'

'So could lots of other officers.'

'But Spider said his boss knows me, and how many police officers have I met in Vancouver?' When some of the doubt left Harrison's face, Tom felt more confident about his evidence. 'Spider thought his boss should have a fancy car. That thing the Inspector drives is like a junk yard on wheels.'

Harrison laughed. 'I think you're prejudiced against the Inspector, but you may have something. What else?'

Tom had planned to mention the Inspector's grumpy attitude, and how he had locked Tom in the cell, but that could also be called prejudice. So he decided to go directly to the reason why he needed Harrison's help.

Tom crossed with Harrison to the other side of the bridge; filled with fear by the long drop, he studied the lighthouse beside the sea wall, far below. 'On Sunday we met Inspector Mort and a work crew at that lighthouse. They claimed to be doing repairs, but that wasn't the truth.'

'Why?'

Tom looked at Harrison. 'Have you read *The Secret of the Caves*?'

'The Hardy Boys book? Yes, but that was years ago.'

'Well, in that book a submarine brings spies in to shore, and they operate out of some caves. I figure there's a secret cave under that lighthouse. Drugs are collected from freighters anchored at sea, then smuggled ashore using an underwater sea scooter, which comes in under the lighthouse. After that Leo and the Inspector use people like Spider to distribute the drugs.'

Harrison was staring at Tom. 'Do you mean that?' he asked, astonished.

'Yes. The Inspector said he'd stopped at the lighthouse during a walk. A guy that fat wouldn't be out walking, and no one does repairs on Sunday, so his gang must have been transferring drugs from the lighthouse into their truck.'

'That's an amazing theory. You certainly have a fantastic imagination, Tom.'

'Thanks, but now I need help, Harrison! We've got to

collect some proof inside that lighthouse, then go straight to the police. The Inspector must be arrested before he can kill me.'

'Kill you?'

'Spider said his boss and Leo were responsible for the death of that police agent. Then, at the railway yards, he told me to say my prayers.'

'I doubt if someone your age would be considered a threat to their operation, Tom, so it's unlikely you're in danger.' Harrison studied Tom, his face serious. 'This fellow Spider sounds like he enjoys being a big talker, so he probably only wanted to scare you.'

'But I could have him arrested.'

'Do you have any actual evidence linking him to drug sales?' When Tom shook his head unhappily, Harrison smiled and squeezed his arm. 'Don't be blue, Tom. You've got a good future, but a detective must always have facts to back up his theories.'

'What about the lighthouse? I'm sure we could find some evidence in there.'

'We can't just break down the door, Tom, and I don't think we could get a search warrant.'

'I guess you're right.' Tom's spirits had plunged to rock bottom, and depression was written all over his face. He had done so much, taken so many risks, and produced nothing. All his great theories were worthless, truly the work of a defective detective.

'Come on,' Harrison said. 'I'll give you a ride home.'

Tom nodded gloomily and turned towards the city coming to life under the soft rays of the sun. At this moment, in that beautiful city, people like Angel were slowly being destroyed by drugs, and Tom had failed them.

'Ready to go?' Harrison asked.

Tom looked at the blond man beside his motorcycle. Sunshine sparkled from the chrome on the rear-view mirror and the fuel cap, stinging Tom's eyes as he tried desperately to think of a way to save his investigation. 'There's one thing I can't figure out.'

'What's that?'

'Spider mentioned something about a cap. He said his boss keeps the drugs inside moisture-proof packages, then has to "fumble with his cap" before he can give the drugs to Spider.'

Harrison looked surprised. 'Perhaps he meant a hat of some sort, Tom.'

Tom's mood brightened. 'Maybe Spider meant Inspector Mort's uniform cap!'

'Possibly,' Harrison said, nodding. 'Let's get going, and we can talk about it later.'

'But why moisture-proof packages?' Tom looked up as a noisy seaplane crossed low over the bridge, splintering the early-morning peace. 'Maybe to protect the drugs in the rain. Or did Spider mean a different kind of cap?'

'I don't know.' Harrison opened up the Harley-Davidson's saddle bag and reached inside, then looked annoyed. 'I haven't got the extra helmet, Tom. You'd better use mine.'

'Then you won't be wearing one,' Tom said. 'Isn't that illegal?'

Harrison shrugged impatiently. 'We'll just have to break the law. I want to take you home, then get some sleep. I've been up all night.'

Tom nodded, and reached across the motorcycle for Harrison's helmet. As he did so, something moved in the shadows of the park, and a man walked quickly on to the bridge.

It was Leo.

Tom's heart jumped as he recognized Leo's evil face, then he looked desperately for somewhere to hide. He took one step towards the bridge's support column, but froze when Leo lifted a gun.

'What's going on?' Harrison demanded, staring at the gun.

Leo ignored Harrison, keeping his cold eyes on Tom as he walked closer. 'You're a real trouble-maker, kid,' he said in his rough voice. 'Now you're going to die.'

'Leave the boy alone,' Harrison said angrily.

'Keep out of this, fool. The kid was going for your cap, and you didn't try to stop him.'

'He was reaching for my helmet, not the cap.'

As the truth dawned on him, Tom stared in shock at Harrison, then turned and dashed to the bridge railing. Scrambling over, he landed on a small platform and grabbed a steel ladder.

'Stop, Tom!' Harrison shouted.

But Tom was already on the ladder and starting down the side of the support column. He heard feet on the platform, and looked up to see Leo's face. The man aimed his gun at Tom, but before he could squeeze the trigger his face twisted in pain.

Harrison had struck Leo's gun hand, and now the two men fought furiously on the tiny platform. Tom clung to the ladder, hearing the men's feet clang against the steel platform and catching glimpses of their struggling bodies, trying to keep terror from overwhelming his mind.

From above came a shout. Tom looked up, and saw the horror in Leo's eyes just before the man tumbled from the platform. A long and sickening cry came from his falling body, and then nothing.

Tom closed his eyes, holding on with all his strength to the steel ladder, trying to forget the terrible cry. At last he looked up, and saw Harrison leaning over the platform.

'Come up now, Tom!' the man called. 'It's safe.'

'No!'

Harrison stared at Tom, then reached for the ladder and started down. Filled with fear, Tom went quickly lower until his feet touched a cross-beam which led off at an angle. Glancing down, he saw the flat surface of the sea, far below.

'Don't look down!' Harrison shouted. A strong wind blew in this exposed space, making Harrison's words sound weak. 'Follow me to the top, one rung at a time.'

'No!'

'Don't be afraid, Tom. You can do it.'

'Confess!' Tom yelled. 'Confess it's you, *you're* Spider's boss!'

'What?' Harrison shouted in disbelief.

'Confess your guilt, then I'll climb up.'

For a long moment, Harrison stared at Tom. 'Are you crazy?'

'Confess!'

When Harrison continued to stare, Tom found the courage to reach his foot towards the cross-beam.

Harrison quickly shook his head. 'Don't do it! Tell me your theory, anything, just don't go lower.'

Tom leaned his head against the ladder and looked at the blue sky; a seagull drifted past, perfectly safe in this loneliness far above the sea. Something tempted him to look down, but he fought off the feeling and raised his eyes to Harrison.

'Show me your sunglasses!'

'OK, sure, anything.' Firmly gripping the ladder,

Harrison reached into his denim jacket. Tom had a glimpse of a silver-coated lens, then Harrison fumbled the sunglasses and they fell straight towards Tom. Closing his eyes, he felt them bounce off his shoulder and fall into the empty sky.

'I'm sorry, Tom!' Harrison yelled. 'It was an accident. I didn't mean to scare you.'

Tom looked up at Harrison. 'There was only one lens! That proves you're Spider's boss.'

'You don't know what you're talking about. I'm starting to climb, Tom. Follow me to the top.' Harrison went up a rung and stopped. 'You must climb. It's your only hope.'

Tom stared at the man, wondering if he planned to escape now that his guilt was exposed. If so, Tom must follow; taking a deep breath, he climbed a rung.

'That's it!' Harrison called. 'Keep climbing.'

Bud's face appeared at the top of the ladder. Tom had completely forgotten about phoning him, and he couldn't believe his eyes. Then he realized he must act quickly.

'Bud!' he yelled. 'Help me!'

'It's OK, Bud,' Harrison shouted. 'I'm leading Tom up, rung by rung.'

'Bud! Open the fuel tank on Harrison's motorcycle and look inside.'

Harrison turned towards Tom, his face shocked. Then he quickly shook his head at Bud. 'Don't do it! The boy's gone crazy.'

'Please, Bud!'

Bud disappeared. Harrison climbed a rung, then seemed to change his mind and started down towards Tom.

Desperately, Tom tried to go lower, but his foot

slipped and dropped into open air. An electric shock of fear passed through him and he clenched the steel rung with all his strength. Closing his eyes, he waited helplessly for Harrison to knock him off the ladder.

'Harrison!'

Bud was calling from above, but Tom lacked the courage to look up. All he could think of was holding on tightly to the ladder.

'Leave him alone, Harrison!' Bud shouted.

A long silence followed, broken at last by the cry of a seagull. Tom slowly lifted his head, and saw Harrison just above him. At the top of the ladder, Bud was leaning over the steel platform, his police revolver aimed at Harrison.

'Climb up, Harrison!' he called. 'You're under arrest.'

'I'm trying to save the kid!'

'Get away from Tom! He can save himself.'

Harrison stared at Tom for a moment, a strange look in his eyes, then went slowly up the ladder. Now Tom realized he was still in terrible danger, and no one could help.

Don't look down, he whispered, Reaching for the next rung with a hand that was suddenly sweaty, he felt his fingers slip on the metal. Closing his eyes, Tom tried to find courage.

'Climb up quickly!'

Bud's voice startled Tom, and for a moment he forgot his fear. Gripping the metal he climbed a rung, then stopped. The wind blew against his body; from somewhere came the sound of a siren. His arms were becoming weak.

'Try again!'

Taking a deep breath, Tom quickly climbed another rung, then stopped and held on tight.

'You've almost made it!'

The wind had become an enemy fighting to tear Tom off the ladder, and even the piercing cries of the seagulls seemed to be trying to scare him into loosening his grip. The siren was loud now, and another seaplane roared over the bridge, adding its noise to the attack on Tom. The whole world is against you, his frightened mind said, you'll never make it to safety.

'You can do it, Tom!'

There was strength in Bud's voice, and a belief that Tom could succeed. Closing his eyes, Tom managed two more rungs and then heard Bud's voice near by.

'You've done it, Tom. Come up to the platform.'

With the last of his energy and courage, Tom climbed higher. Strong hands gripped his shoulders, then he was lying on the steel platform, his body shaking.

'It's all over,' Bud said quietly. 'You're safe now.'

Gradually, the shaking died away. Feeling terribly tired, Tom got slowly to his feet and climbed over the railing.

Everything looked different. A police car was on the bridge, emergency lights spinning, and Harrison sat inside it under guard. Two officers stood beside Harrison's motorcycle, one of them holding the fuel cap. Hanging from the bottom of the cap was a long plastic tube, with a number of packages inside it.

When Tom reached the police car, Harrison looked out of the window and shook his head.

'I was wrong,' he said.

'What about?' Tom asked, still frightened of the man.

'When Spider warned us that you were a threat, I laughed at him.' Harrison's blue eyes studied Tom's face. 'But I still tried to keep you out of harm, Tom. After your phone call, Leo insisted that we find out how much you knew, but I managed to get him to wait in hiding at the end of the bridge. I wanted to get you away before he could hurt you.'

Tom stared at him, wondering if he was speaking the truth. It was something Tom would never know for sure, but right now he was too upset to care. Turning, he walked away.

10

During the next few days Tom was busy talking to police investigators about Harrison and Spider, both of whom were under arrest.

Then Nanny and Gramps decided it was time for a picnic. Dietmar and his relatives were invited, and Tom returned to Shanghai Alley to see if ZZ would come, but she had gone to Radium Hot Springs to visit her family.

Everyone gathered at Third Beach on the west side of Stanley Park. Happily, Lions Gate Bridge was not visible from here, and Tom was completely relaxed as he and Dietmar whipped a Frisbee back and forth.

'Time to eat!' Nanny called, waving from a blanket spread out beside a log on the beach. Beyond her was the sea wall, and the park's tall trees.

Tom flipped the Frisbee a final time, watching it shoot past Dietmar's outstretched hands to a landing near the sea. Grinning, he waited for Dietmar to fetch the Frisbee before they walked back towards the waiting food.

Spread out on the blanket was a feast of hot dogs and hamburgers, salads and pop. 'Where's the dessert?' Dietmar asked, sitting down on the sand.

Gramps smiled. 'That's a surprise for later. But meanwhile here's a riddle for you: a man who lives in a cabin with four identical walls, each of which faces south, sees a bear walk past outside his window. What colour is the bear?'

A puzzled silence followed. Tom, who had heard the riddle, studied a fishing boat heading towards the harbour, a tangled pattern of ropes running between the mast and the big nets on its deck. A heron was swimming closer to shore, its head and long curved neck forming a question mark above the waves.

'Is the bear white?' Dietmar's aunt asked uncertainly.

'Excellent!' Gramps said. 'Why?'

'Well, the cabin must be standing right on the North Pole for all the walls to face south, so it would be a polar bear going past.'

'Give the lady a free hot dog,' Gramps said, smiling.

Dietmar's uncle looked at Tom. 'May I ask you something?'

'Sure,' Tom said. 'Is it a riddle?'

'No, but it's a puzzle to me. While you were throwing the Frisbee, the rest of us discussed your drugs investigation. But, tell me, how did you know on the bridge that Harrison was Spider's boss?'

'I suddenly realized there was a fuel cap on Harrison's motorcycle, and the moisture-proof packages could be hidden beneath the cap, in the fuel tank.

And I also remembered the litter on the shack floor.'

'Yes?'

'There were cigar butts in the litter, and Harrison is a cigar-smoker. I also saw a broken lens, and realized later that Harrison's sunglasses had probably fallen out of his pocket and been broken when Spider was being beaten up in the shack.'

'Have some more pop?' Nanny asked.

'Thanks Nanny,' Tom said, holding out his cup. 'I knew that Harrison left the police force to make more money, yet I didn't realize that gave me his motive for selling drugs. Not only that, we met a girl named Angel after our motorcycle ride and Harrison called her one of his customers. At the time I thought he was trying to help her, but in fact he must have been selling her drugs.'

'I'm also puzzled about something,' Nanny said. 'How did this Harrison person obtain inside information about police activities?'

'I suppose because he hung around in the Police Club talking to the officers who were his friends it wasn't difficult for him to get information.' For a moment, Tom thought about his visit to the club, and his ride on Harrison's motorcycle. 'I guess Spider didn't think much of motorcycles.'

'What do you mean?' Gramps asked.

'He said his boss should have a fancy car.' Tom smiled. 'Obviously he meant Harrison, but that remark started me after a different suspect.'

'Who?'

Tom was about to answer, but paused when he spotted a familiar figure approaching along the sea wall. 'Isn't that Inspector Mort?' he said, staring at a fat man in a track suit who was puffing from the strain of a long run.

'You're right, Tom,' Gramps said, standing up to wave. 'Over here, Inspector!'

Looking relieved, the Inspector paused to catch his breath before coming slowly across the sand. 'Good afternoon,' he said, sitting down on the log and taking out a big handkerchief to mop his red face. 'I don't think I'm ready for the Olympic team.'

Gramps laughed, and introduced the Inspector to Dietmar's relatives. 'I'm sure you remember Tom and Dietmar,' he added.

'I certainly do,' the Inspector said, putting away his handkerchief. 'That's why I'm here today.'

'Are you going to arrest Tom?' Dietmar asked hopefully.

'No,' the Inspector said, smiling. 'In fact, I've come to thank Tom for the help he gave our police force, and to apologize for locking him in a cell. I was wrong to think he needed a little scare to keep him from getting into trouble.'

'That's OK,' Dietmar said, 'but now Tom wants to try being locked up for a couple of years.'

The Inspector held out his hand. 'No hard feelings?'

'No, sir,' Tom said, shaking his hand. 'I guess I made a couple of mistakes about you, too.'

'Oh? Like what?'

'Nothing much,' Tom said, unwilling to mention his theory about the lighthouse. When it was clear that everyone was waiting for an answer, he added, 'I thought you weren't the type to walk around the park, let alone run.'

The Inspector laughed. 'I'm trying to lose weight,' he said. 'I guess I'm too fond of tying on the feed bag.'

'Speaking of food,' Dietmar said, 'I wonder when we're going to be surprised with our dessert.'

94

'It's arriving by road,' the Inspector said. Turning, he pointed at a figure emerging between the thick trees of the park. 'Here comes the delivery, and right on time.'

'It's Bud!' Tom said, recognizing the officer as he crossed the beach, a cardboard container in his hands.

'Hi there,' Bud said, as he put down the container. 'Hey, Inspector, this stuff is cold.'

'That's how ice-cream should be,' the Inspector said, smiling when Tom and Dietmar looked at him with delighted faces. 'It's a special gift from the Vancouver City Police.'

'Fantastic!' Dietmar said. 'What flavour?'

'Something special, and I had to search all over town to find it.' The Inspector opened the container, revealing bright blue ice-cream. 'Your grandparents tell me you're a big fan of Dubble Bubble, Tom.'

'Yes, sir,' Tom said. Feeling uncertain, he took a spoon and tasted a bit of ice-cream, then grinned. 'Great!' he said, smiling at the Inspector. 'Thanks a million!'

Dietmar watched Tom dig into the container, his face suspicious. Finally, as the ice-cream rapidly began to disappear, he tried a bit himself. 'It's Bubble Gum ice-cream!' he said, staring at the Inspector, then quickly concentrated on getting his share.

When it was gone, Tom and Dietmar lay back on the sand with bright blue mouths, staring at the sky while their stomachs worked busily. After a while, Tom sat up and looked out to sea, watching waves leap up around a freighter as it headed towards the late-afternoon sun.

'I wonder if that's the *MK Maru*,' he said.

'No, it's not,' the Inspector answered. 'I said good-bye to Captain Yakashi a few days ago.'

'Did you ever catch those drug smugglers?'

95

'We were never after smugglers,' the Inspector said, smiling, 'but we obtained some valuable information about illegal immigrants.'

'I was so certain I could round up a whole bunch of smugglers,' said Tom glumly. 'Catching Harrison and Spider doesn't seem much in comparison.'

'Catching them was extremely important. In addition, it turns out Harrison and Leo operated a large ring, and we arrested several more of their people today. That's all thanks to your work, young man.'

'Hey!' Dietmar said. 'I just remembered something!'

'What?' Tom asked, suspicious of the sudden delight on Dietmar's face.

'When I heard Captain Yakashi's name, I started thinking about The Breadline restaurant. Remember what you said, Tom, when you first saw Inspector Mort?'

Tom remembered, but he didn't want to. 'How about tossing the Frisbee?' he said, standing up quickly.

'Wait a minute!' Dietmar said happily. Looking at Inspector Mort, he grinned. 'Tom said he'd eat his hat if you weren't a crook.'

'A crook?' the Inspector said, frowning.

'I'm sorry,' Tom said, his face turning bright red. 'I guess we all make mistakes.'

Dietmar pulled a baseball cap out of Tom's hip pocket and dropped it on a plate. 'Want some salt?'

'Hold on!' Tom said. 'I didn't really mean I'd eat it.'

'You were lying?' Dietmar said, shaking his head in sorrow. 'That's hard to believe, Tom.'

Inspector Mort reached forward. 'I owe you a favour, Tom,' he said, picking up the cap. Before anyone could speak, he put a corner of the cap in his mouth and his big teeth closed around the fabric.